Horse Mad Western

P9-AQP-763

Horse Mad
Western

Kathy Helidoniotis

WALRUS
B O O K S

Copyright © Kathy Helidoniotis 2008.

Walrus Books, an imprint of Whitecap Books

All rights reserved. No part of this publication may be reproduced, stored in a retrieval system, or transmitted in any form or by any means, electronic, mechanical, photocopying, recording, or otherwise, without the prior written permission of the publisher.

This edition published in North America in 2009 by Whitecap Books Ltd. For more information, contact Whitecap Books, 351 Lynn Avenue, North Vancouver, British Columbia, Canada V7J 2C4. Visit our website at www.whitecap.ca.

First published in English in Sydney, Australia by HarperCollins Publishers Australia Pty Limited in 2008. This edition is published by arrangement with HarperCollins Publishers Australia Pty Limited.

The author has asserted their right to be identified as the author of this work.

Library and Archives Canada Cataloguing in Publication

Helidoniotis, Kathy
    Horse mad western / Kathy Helidoniotis.

ISBN 978-1-55285-996-4

    1. Horses--Juvenile fiction. I. Title.

PZ7.H374How 2009   j823'.92   C2009-902690-2

The publisher acknowledges the financial support of the Canada Council for the Arts, the British Columbia Arts Council, and the Government of Canada through the Book Publishing Industry Development Program (BPIDP). Whitecap Books also acknowledges the financial support of the Province of British Columbia through the Book Publishing Tax Credit.

Canada Council Conseil des Arts
for the Arts du Canada

BRITISH COLUMBIA
ARTS COUNCIL

Printed in Canada.

09 10 11 12 13   5 4 3 2 1

For Mariana, John and Simon,
with all my love,
and for Seb, with all my heart.

G'day Mate!

This story takes place in Australia — so if you want to brush up on your Aussie slang (what is a 'brumby'?), just flip to the helpful glossary at the back of the book.

one

Howdy, Pardner!

'It's on again, people!' Gary Cho stood on his dusty blue milk crate and beamed at the members of Shady Creek Riding Club. Gary is the most awesome Riding Club instructor anywhere in the world. 'The fourteenth annual Pinebark Ridge Western Riding Club Show is on in eight weeks.'

'Cool!' I murmured, rubbing my fingers in my gorgeous chestnut mare's soft copper-coloured mane. I'd never done any Western riding. But I never let details like that stop me. Once I knew there was a show on I wanted in. The events of the last year trooped through my head like a slide show. I'd ridden mounted games and cross-country, and I'd even tried dressage. And I'd loved every single minute of every single event. As long as I was riding, I was happy.

I leaned forward in my saddle and wrapped my arms around Honey's firm neck. She's my hero. Since the day I found her abandoned and half-starved on the run-down farm that became Shady Trails Riding Ranch (my second favourite place in the world, after Riding Club!) we've been inseparable.

I closed my eyes and breathed in Honey's warm horsy smell. I could see it all. Honey and I are in the ring. I'm wearing a cowgirl hat so pure white it's giving off its own light. My pink-sequined, long-sleeved Western shirt with the long pointy collars is buttoned up to my neck and I've got the coolest brown leather chaps. We're loping around the ring and the crowd is cheering. I swing my lariat above my head, around and around and around, and then I let fly and whammo! I've roped myself a—

'Ashleigh Miller! Is your position in the saddle acceptable at Riding Club?'

I sat bolt upright. 'No, Gary,' I said, shaking my head.

Gary frowned and folded his arms. 'Would you remind us exactly what constitutes an acceptable rider's position?'

I swallowed, feeling fourteen pairs of eyes boring into my very skin like lasers, and I wasn't enjoying it one bit.

'The rider should sit in a balanced vertical position. You should be able to draw an imaginary line from your shoulder to your hip and down to your heel.'

Gary smiled. 'Perfect. Perhaps now you could tell us why a rider should never be slumped forward in the saddle whispering sweet nothings in their horse's ear?'

Some of the Shady Creek riders giggled. My cheeks burned and I cast Becky Cho a pitiful look. Becky is Gary's daughter, my best friend and the hottest rider around. She gave me a sympathetic smile and chewed on her bottom lip. Her amazing bay, part-Arab gelding, Charlie, shook his head, scolding me.

'It's dangerous,' I said. My voice was small. I hated being caught out making a mistake. I hated it even more when my mistake was in full view of Flea Fowler, Carly Barnes and Ryan Thomas, the dreaded Three Creepketeers, my sworn enemies. They've hated me since the day I arrived in Shady Creek from our old place in the city, and believe me the feeling is totally mutual. They hate Becky, too. It's hard when your dad is the instructor. Some kids get silly ideas about favouritism.

I tried to control the urge, but I just couldn't help myself. I sent a sly peek in the direction of the Creepketeers. They were all eyes and ears and loving every minute of my roasting. Carly was doing some kind of victory dance in her saddle. Her sweet white mare, Destiny, twisted her head around to gaze up at her mistress. Carly just didn't deserve her.

'If Honey bolted or shied I'd probably fall. I wouldn't have time to save myself or bring her under control.'

'Exactamundo,' Gary said. 'Now back to the show.'

I sighed, totally relieved, but shifted in my saddle until my seat was perfect. If there was one thing I could thank Waratah Grove Riding Academy for it was intensive training in acquiring the perfect seat.

'I just got the program this morning. It's so hot off the press I fried my breakfast eggs on it!'

Gary watched us expectantly, waiting for our sides to split.

Riding Club meetings often start with Gary making a terrible joke that nobody thinks is funny. They do untold damage to Becky's psychological health. She buried her face in her gloved hands, whimpering. I leaned over in my saddle and patted her back. Honey stamped and tossed her head. It's so totally unreal the way she always knows how I'm feeling. That's one of the reasons I love her so much.

'So what?' Carly, Queen Creepketeer, looped her reins around her arm and smoothed down her red hair. I fumed.

Why had I been fried for my one teeny-weeny mistake and Carly could loop her reins around her arm? That's one of the most dangerous things you can do on horseback. I pointed at her and opened my mouth, ready to strike.

'None of us ride Western, Gary,' Carly said, before I had my chance. 'Why should we care?'

Gary's face flushed, but he said nothing. I wasn't surprised at the way his jaw suddenly clenched.

'*I* ride Western.' Flea scratched underneath his dark blue Riding Club polo shirt and flashed a set of grimy teeth. He's the grottiest boy I've ever met, a committed Creepketeer and, unfortunately, my next-door neighbour.

'And I'm counting on you to help,' Gary said.

'Me?' Flea puffed out his chest, blew on his fingernails and rubbed them on his shirt. It was probably the first polish they'd had in years.

Gary nodded, shading his eyes from the sun with his hand. His tattered blue Riding Club cap was missing in action. Either he'd left it at home or it had finally disintegrated. 'I want everyone to have a go. You're all great riders, brilliant, in fact. But no rider, no matter how good, should ever rest on their lucerne.'

Becky moaned and rolled her eyes. 'He's getting worse!'

'I thought we'd agreed that was impossible,' I whispered, shaking my head.

'You need a challenge,' Gary continued. 'And what better challenge than learning a new way of riding?'

'How new?' I said. I figured getting serious about Western riding might weaken, or at least temporarily distract, his urge to crack rotten jokes.

'Over the next few weeks you'll be trained in basic Western riding skills like neck-reining, and the more advanced riders may learn the Sliding Halt and Rollback.'

'Huh?' Eleven-year-old Jodie Ferguson scrunched up her face in bewilderment. Her identical twin sister, Julie, did the same.

'Don't worry, you'll soon learn the lingo.' Gary pulled a crumpled show program out of the back pocket of his jeans and waved it in the air. 'Anyway, some of the events will be very familiar to you.' Gary flicked through the pages. 'Like barrel racing.'

'Yes!' I bounced in my saddle and high-fived Becky. I love barrel racing. There's nothing on the planet that does it for me like barrel racing. Except maybe cross-country riding. And dressage. And mounted games and hacks and horse-swimming. Come to think of it, everything about horses does it for me. I suppose that's to be expected when you're totally, fully, utterly, hopelessly horse mad! I was so stoked it didn't even bother me when Carly rolled her eyes and pretended to throw up.

'What else?' Sandra stroked the neck of her dark brown pony, Chocolate, then sneezed so hard I was sure Jenna would have heard her in Italy. Sandra's so allergic to horses she hardly ever comes to Riding Club. Jenna's my best friend from the city. She'd been living overseas for months and I couldn't wait for her to come home.

Gary peered at the pages. 'There's Campdrafting and Steer Undecorating for advanced riders. And there are always Showmanship and Halter classes, Western Pleasure and novelty events like biggest horse, smallest horse and—'

'Dumbest horse?' Carly said, sneering. 'There'll be no competition. Spiller's mule'll win, hands down.'

Carly and I don't exactly get along. In fact, the day I become Prime Minister is the day I outlaw Carly and 'Spiller Miller', my dreaded nickname.

I stiffened and opened my mouth, so ready to bite back my teeth were tingling. Nobody says stuff like that about my Honey and rides away with it. Becky pressed her finger to her lips and shook her head. I sighed. She was right. Carly is so not worth it.

'Another comment like that, Carly, and you're pooper-scooping the corral.' Gary's eyes were like slits. 'By yourself.'

I beamed at Becky who stifled giggles. Carly made a strange choking noise, like she was desperately forcing a long stream of nasty words back down her throat.

Gary pointed at another page of the program. 'You can try your hands at Showmanship and Hunter Under Saddle. Most of you would easily qualify for the beginner classes.' Gary took a breath and smiled at the Shady Creek riders. I stared at him, blankly. This was all so new. Hunter Under Saddle? Sliding Halt? What did it all mean?

'Flea, can you tell us a little about riding Western?' Gary said.

'It's a really old form of riding,' Flea said. He was enthusiastic. The most enthusiastic he'd been since seeing me fall off Honey during a cross-country training session. 'It was brought to America by the Spanish and made its way to the Wild West.'

I stared at Flea, my mouth open. He'd never said anything that intelligent before. I hated to admit it, but I was impressed.

'Western riders sit for the walk, jog and lope and ...'

'What's a jog?' Julie burst out.

'What's a lope?' Jodie slapped her hand over her mouth. The twins giggled feverishly.

I waited for Flea to bite their heads clean off. Or pelt them with horse poo at the very least. But he smiled instead. It was creepy.

'The jog is the Western trot and the lope is the canter. They're much slower than the English paces.'

'Oh,' the twins said together, looking as stunned by Flea's sudden personality switch as I felt. Becky and I exchanged awe-struck glances.

'What about that one-handed rein thing?' Ryan called. 'I've seen it on TV.'

Flea rolled his eyes. 'That's neck-reining, you idiot.'

Chatter erupted in the lines like clanging lids. Becky and I smiled at one another. The real Flea was still in there.

Gary clapped his hands twice, his signal to be quiet and focus. 'I want a ten-minute warm-up. Laps of the ring at a trot for five then serpentines at a canter for three and figure eights for two. Got that?'

We all nodded and urged our horses and ponies towards the warm-up ring. Some riders hate the warm-up. They think it's boring. But I love it. Not only is it necessary for a horse to be warm and supple before a ride or training, it's also the best time to really concentrate on your horse. To listen to their hooves pounding and feel their heart beating faster and faster under the saddle. It's a time to think about your seat and fuse your body into your horse's, to be so close to this other being that you can no longer separate yourselves.

Honey and I completed our laps at a trot. Gary prefers a trot for most of our warm-ups. He often says it suits the whole club, from beginners to the most advanced riders, and is a comfortable pace for the horses. Gary clapped twice. The five minutes at a trot was up. We moved to a canter for serpentines, or S-shapes. The warm-up ring was large enough for two groups to work at separate serpentines at the same time. Gary clapped his hands again and called for figure eights.

Once warm-up was finished we settled back into our lines, according to our age groups. Under 10s first, then Under 12s, Under 14s, Under 18s then Opens, where riders can be up to twenty-five years old, but there are only a few of them. Most Open riders are sleeping in on Sunday mornings.

Lining up makes everything (inspection, training, games) easier for Gary, but Becky and I suffer horribly every single meeting. Now that we have two Under-12 teams we have to line up beside the Creepketeers, ride with them and against them and to top it off, we're all in the same class at school. I knew Shady Creek was a small town before we moved here, but I had never expected it to be this small!

'To begin with I'd like to teach you the most basic Western technique of all,' Gary said. 'The Western seat.'

'Bor-ing!' Carly sang.

'We weren't talking about you, Carly. We were talking about the Western seat.' Becky smiled sweetly at Carly whose face turned more red than her hair.

'Zip your lip, Rebecca's Garden,' Carly hissed, out of Gary's earshot. She's mean but she's not silly.

Becky's eyes narrowed. She is totally over being teased about her parents' Chinese restaurant. 'Call me that again and I'll be zipping yours.'

Carly threw back her head and laughed. 'Ooh, I'm really scared. We're all scared, aren't we?'

Flea snorted. 'I'm shaking. How about you, Ry?'

'Huh?' Ryan Thomas looked around. He's pretty harmless most of the time, when he isn't following Flea and Carly around and doing all the dumb things they tell him to, that is.

'Enough chatter!' Gary bellowed. 'Western seats!'

I was determined to learn as much as I could about Western riding and ignore the Creepketeers.

'A Western rider sits vertically with a back that is straight, not arched, and as with English riding there should be that famous imaginary line that Ashleigh reminded us about earlier.' Gary gave me a small wink. I frowned at him, pressing my lips together so tight it hurt. I learned that trick from my mum.

'Flea, front and centre.'

Flea grinned, saluted Gary, and Scud stepped out of the line.

'I want to demonstrate the Western seat on Flea.' Gary patted Scud's sleek black neck and the horse's eyes narrowed. I wasn't sure if he was relaxed or seriously considering biting Gary on the backside.

'Everyone watch Flea. See the vertical, imaginary line.' Flea sat tall and proud. 'His legs are bent slightly at the knee and his weight is dropped into his heel. The leg position is longer than for English riding. His seat is tucked under. You need to be sitting deeply.' Gary turned to us and smiled. 'You soak up the horse's movements. That's how the Western rider sits for all gaits — paces. Got it?'

There were some murmured replies. We got it. All we had to do now was flaunt it.

'The reins are held in one hand and the rider steers the horse by laying the reins on the horse's neck. Western reins are split so—'

'What's split?' Julie waved her hand frantically.

'They don't join up in the middle like English reins. There's no buckle. They're heaps longer, too.'

'Oh.' Julie nodded slowly. 'Should I just unbuckle my reins?'

'Nuh.' Flea shook his head. 'Won't make any difference. You don't have enough rein to hold them Western-style.'

Gary patted Scud's nose and stepped back to admire his star Western rider. 'Look and learn everyone — the perfect Western seat.'

The Shady Creek riders applauded and Flea seemed pleased. Gary spent the next hour moulding, squishing and pushing us into the perfect Western seat, then told us all about holding the reins in our right or left hand, whichever we were most comfortable with, and getting our horses' heads to drop. It seemed so different to everything I'd ever known. My English riding teachers had always stressed how important it was to keep a short rein and be in firm contact with a horse's mouth. I'd always tried to bring Honey's head up.

But by the end of the day I'd been so badly bitten by the Western bug I was craving beans, bootscootin' and singing cowgirl songs.

'What d'you reckon about Western?' Becky asked, as we made our way home from Riding Club. It's never too far for me. I live on the same street.

'Well, pardner,' I said. 'I reckon it's awesome. Hey, you're using both hands, Beck. We pinky swore to hold the reins in one hand all the way home.'

Becky sighed. 'Not fair. You only have to ride a few

metres. I have to do it for a few blocks. I'm gonna wind up in Pinebark Ridge the way I'm going.'

'No way. If you ride Western half as well as you ride everything else you'll be *fantastico*!'

'Speaking of *fantastico*, heard from Jenna?' Becky glared at her hands. I could tell that every fibre of her being was screaming at her to ride English. It's not easy ignoring the English habit of a lifetime.

'A while ago,' I said. When she'd first gone to Italy with her mum and brothers I'd got an email from Jenna every day. Then when she'd started going to school there I heard from her every week. Now I was lucky to hear from her once a fortnight. It wasn't like her.

'D'you reckon her parents'll get back together?'

I shook my head. 'Not a chance. That's why she's in Italy, remember? Her mum wanted to stay with her family for a while to help her get over it. Jenna's dad's got his own place now and everything. Jenna reckons he might even have a girlfriend.'

Becky was solemn. 'Wow. They must really be finished. Is Jenna okay with that?'

'She's getting used to it,' I said.

Becky pulled Charlie up outside my place. 'This is your stop. See you at school tomorrow.'

'Ring you tonight?' I held out my hand and Becky clasped it, hard.

'You're on.' She pulled Charlie's head up and urged him into a trot, both hands on her reins.

'Cheat!' I called after her, then turned Honey into our driveway and let go of my reins, completely giving her her head. Honey's head dropped and she walked slowly into the corral.

I slid to the ground. 'Fast learner.'

She twisted her head around and rubbed her sweet face against my shoulder. I wrapped my arms around her neck and buried my face in her mane.

'This is gonna be so cool, Honey horse,' I murmured. 'So totally cool.'

two

Project B & B

'TOYS!'

I was so shocked by my mother's sudden and most unwelcome entrance into my bedroom, I almost fell from my chair.

'What's wrong with you?'

Mum was standing in the doorway panting. Her hair was wild, like a crop of tumbleweed, and her fists were clenched at her sides. She looked like she hadn't eaten, slept or washed in a month.

'Toys!' Mum gulped. 'Need old toys. For guest playroom. You give me.'

I glared at her and folded my arms. 'Don't have old toys. Parents forced me to chuck out before left city.'

'Arrrgh!' Mum slapped her hands over her face. 'Oh, Ash. Haven't you got a few dollies or something? The playroom's so empty it looks like a prison and you know we can't afford to buy new things.'

I gave her a look, my arms still crossed fiercely over my chest.

'C'mon, Ash.' Mum charged at my walk-in wardrobe. 'You hoard like a bowerbird. I know you smuggled all those board games to Shady Creek. You never use them.'

I sniffed and turned back to my homework. Now that I'm in Year Six I have a lot to do. There's reading and spelling and Maths and Science and the whole class is doing a special study of the world's deadliest snakes. I am not at all happy that most of them live right here in Australia. 'How can I play them by myself? You guys are always too busy and Jason'd just eat the pieces.'

'You won't miss them, then.' Mum rummaged around for a few minutes and emerged with a stack of my favourite old games — the ones Jenna and I used to play together on rainy days. Just seeing them made me miss her.

'Where exactly is the guest playroom?' I asked as

casually as I could. The truth was I was getting a little fed up with the B & B. So far we'd lost two spare rooms and the bathroom upstairs and the TV room downstairs. I was expecting my own bedroom to be room-jacked the minute my back was turned. I'd caught Mum sending thoughtful looks in the direction of my ensuite since the day they'd decided to open Miller Lodge.

Mum made a noise that sounded like 'hubble bubble'.

'Where?' I spun around on my chair and raised one eyebrow, a look I'd learned from Mum. I only hoped I was as terrifying as she could be.

'That spare room, by the pool. You know the pool? That huge rectangular hole in the ground with water in it that you never use.'

I glowered. 'I do so use it!'

Mum slid a few paces closer to my bookshelf. 'I can count on one hand the times you've used it. By the way, it's been a week since I asked you to clean it. We need all the frogs out before the guests arrive.' She scrutinized a row of books. 'Surely you don't read these any more.'

I sprang from my chair, ready to rescue anything Mum had her eye on. 'First, I'd like to see you count anything on one hand right now. Second, you're not allowed to take even one single thing from my horse collection, and that includes books!'

Mum sighed sharply through very pursed lips and launched into a fresh stream of 'hubble bubbling'.

I hovered behind Mum. 'What are you talking about?'

Carefully balancing everything in one arm, Mum slipped an old picture book about a bunny from my shelf and slapped it on top of the pile of games. 'If you're not going to donate, the very least you could do is help your father and me.'

I slapped my hands against my forehead. 'I've got homework to do! Haven't you always said that homework comes first?'

Mum waved her empty hand, as though my homework was the least of her worries. 'We need all Miller hands on deck.'

'But it's due tomorrow!' I wailed.

Mum jerked her head in the direction of my bedroom door. 'We'll give you a hand later on.'

'But you've always said I have to do my homework on my own. How am I ever gonna learn if I don't try things out for myself and make a few mistakes?'

Mum's face went red. 'We're opening soon. We need your help.'

I looked into her eyes, which were colder than Shady Creek in winter, and scuttled from my room into the chaos of the hallway.

Dad's ladder was propped on its side against the wall and there were tins of paint, paint trays, spotty old drop sheets and brushes scattered about.

'Whaddya want me to do?' I asked, sighing.

Mum pointed down the hallway to the ex-spare bedroom. It had been claimed by Miller Lodge as Guest Room 1. I could make out the distinctive sound of paint rollers swooshing across walls.

'Help your father out for a while, please, poss?' Mum gave me her sweetest smile and shooed me down the hall. I had the feeling that the minute I disappeared from view she'd pounce on my room and relieve me of the possessions that she believed I no longer required.

I knocked on the door of Guest Room 1. 'Need any help?'

Dad's face was red, beneath a thick splattering of powder-blue paint. 'You bet!' He handed me his roller brush. 'Knock yourself out. Up and down strokes only, please, Picasso.'

'What if I like side to side?'

Dad grimaced. 'You'll be up and downing over your side to siding, that's what!'

I dipped the roller into a paint tray and gave it a thump on the lip, just as I'd seen Dad do. Then I pressed it to the wall and rolled it up and down, trying hard not to leave gaps of the white undercoat showing. Dad rolled on the wall behind me. After a while I said, 'Why this colour?'

'*Blue is an excellent bedroom colour because it makes one feel comforted and serene.* Don't you want our guests to feel comforted and serene?'

'Where'd you get that from?' I wrinkled my nose. Wet paint isn't exactly my aroma of choice. Wet horse is much better.

Dad laughed. 'Colour chart. You pleased about the B & B?'

'Sure,' I said, dipping my roller back into the tray.

The truth is I wasn't so sure. Mum wasn't working. Dad was taking time off. Jason still seemed so new. I had two equine mouths to feed, so I knew about money. I'd learned a long time ago that it didn't grow on trees and I was almost totally convinced there were no pots of gold at the bottom of any rainbows. There were so many things I wanted, needed to ask him. But when I saw the hope in his eyes and the paint splatters on his face, I pushed all my questions down to the very pit of my stomach.

Later that night, as I lay in bed, those questions haunted me. What if nobody stayed at our B & B? What if we ran out of money? What if the hospital liked the new Nurse Unit Manager better than Dad and they took his job away? What if Mum never went back to plumbing? What would happen to us? And worse, the scariest question of them all, what would happen to Honey and Toff?

The answers were written on the wall, but unlike the undercoat, three coats of paint were not going to make them go away.

The B & B could be the worst mistake we had ever made and if it was, it could mean saying goodbye to Shady Creek forever.

three

Secret Cowboy

'Where didja say you found this?'

We were lying on our stomachs on Becky's bedroom floor, poring over an old photo album.

'Rachael's room,' Becky said absentmindedly as she ran her index finger across the old plastic pages. They crinkled back at her. 'Under her mattress. Thanks for coming over, by the way. I know you've got work and everything but I just *had* to show you.'

'You look under Rachael's mattress?'

Becky stared at me, like I was someone very strange. 'Course I do. And the nanosecond Jason's strong enough to lift it, he'll be looking under yours, too.'

I frowned. 'But what were you looking for?'

Becky grinned. 'Anything.'

The album was filled with pictures of a baby-faced Gary wearing a Stetson hat, jeans and a belt buckle the size of a small planet. He was mounted on a stunning chestnut gelding whose powerful forelegs had the look of a Quarter Horse. This was as much a surprise to Becky as it was to me. It seemed she'd been living with an undercover Western rider for twelve years and hadn't had a clue.

'He's never said a thing to you about riding Western?'

Becky shook her head, frowning. 'Not a word. I feel weird looking at these. It's like I'm reading his diary or something.'

'Look,' I tapped at a photo. 'He's rounding up cows.'

'You really are Western-challenged, aren't you?' Becky rolled her eyes. 'That's cutting.'

'Who are you to talk?' I cried.

'I grew up in the country, remember? I've been to a rodeo or two in my time.' Becky sighed.

'Oh,' I turned another page. It crinkled at me, like the last thing it had wanted to do was be turned. 'D'you reckon he still has this stuff?'

Becky shrugged, squinting at a photo of Gary mounted on the chestnut in front of an enormous sign that said: *National Western Riding Association*. He looked happy. His horse looked like a champion. 'I can't believe this. He's never even hinted he knew about Western. You saw him at Riding Club. I had the feeling he knew more than he was letting on.'

I was confused. 'But why would he be asking Flea for riding advice?'

'Dunno.' Becky scratched her chin. 'But I guess that would explain Bonnie!'

'Bonnie?' I frowned.

'You know Bonnie, his mare?'

I elbowed Becky. 'Duh.'

'Don't you get it, Ash?' Becky's eyes were wide. She sat up in a flurry of arms and legs, like she just couldn't lie down and enlighten me at the same time. 'Bonnie's a Pinto.'

I shrugged. 'So?'

Becky slapped her hands against her forehead and moaned. 'The Pinto or Paint Horse has always been associated with the American West.'

'You've been eating horse books for breakfast again, haven't you?'

'Ashleigh!' Becky wailed. 'Bonnie's a Western

horse. I dunno why I never realized it before. I mean I always knew it but I didn't realize it. Know what I'm saying?'

'No,' I said, so confused my head felt like it was stuffed full of tumbleweed. 'What are you saying?'

'I'm saying he's been riding a Western horse since as long as I can remember. And here he is in all these photos dressed like someone out of a John Wayne movie. My dad was a Western rider and he's never told me.' Becky turned another page over in the album. Gary smiled up at us from the yellowed pages. His horse stood proud and strong, a thick Reserve Champion ribbon tied around its neck. 'I just want to know why. And I want Rachael to spill everything she knows. I mean, what's this doing in her room?'

I thought for a moment. 'But she'll find out you were snooping.'

Becky's face flushed. 'Great!'

'Where's our favourite big sister, anyway?'

'She left really early this morning for Shady Trails.'

I glanced up quickly at the clock on Becky's wall. 'But we don't need to be there for another hour.'

'I hardly see her since Mrs McMurray, well — you know.'

We both knew the only good thing to have come from Cassata's theft was Rachael finally coming to her senses. Boys and icky make-up were out and horses were back in. We owed Mrs Mac big time.

'Ready to go?'

Becky nodded. 'Yep.'

She scooped up the album and I followed her to Rachael's bedroom. I'd never been inside it before. Rachael had made sure of that. My tummy bubbled with fear as I helped Becky lift her sister's mattress, replace the album exactly where she'd found it, and made sure the bed was just as unmade as Rachael had left it. 'For a rainy day,' she said.

Our horses were waiting. I'd ridden Honey to Becky's place, untacked her and tucked her into the corral with a haynet. It was empty now and flapped in the breeze. I shivered in my riding boots. 'It's so cold, here. It was never this cold in the city.'

'I seem to remember you saying the exact same thing about summer.' Becky called out to Charlie and the gelding lifted his head from the patch of lush grass he was munching. 'Except you whined that it was too hot.'

'Well, it's true,' I grumbled, unlatching the corral gate. 'My fingers are turning blue.'

Honey took a few steps towards me. She stretched out her neck and touched her nose to my hands, searching for a treat. I pulled a slice of carrot out of my jacket pocket. Mum reckons I've got a veggie patch growing in there. I wish I did — it would certainly help lower Horse Cents' average weekly expenditure. I offered Honey the carrot, my palm outstretched and flat and my fingers well away from her teeth.

I unhooked my bridle from the peg outside the corral and, approaching my gorgeous mare from her nearside, slipped the reins over her neck, resting them on her poll. I slid the headpiece of the bridle up over Honey's nose and held the bit against her mouth with my left hand. Once the bit was securely in her mouth, I pulled the headpiece of the bridle up over her ears, checked that her mane and forelock weren't caught and buckled her throatlatch (making sure there was a hand's width between it and her throat) and her noseband.

I had unsaddled Honey to give her a chance to rest and relax in the Chos' corral before our hack to Shady Trails. It also meant there was no chance of my saddle being rubbed against the wooden fence and being ruined. But now I had to saddle her up again.

'Race ya?' Becky called, holding Charlie's saddle over her left arm. The gelding stretched his head forward, taking a good long sniff of the soft brown leather.

I shook my head. 'Rebecca Cho, I am disgusted. Safety and correctly tacking up your horse are much more important than how fast you do it.'

Becky grinned at me. 'Ready?'

Call me weak, but I couldn't resist a horse challenge. 'You bet.'

We counted to three and burst into action. Honey's saddle blanket was in position a little further up on her withers than it needed to be in the flick of a pony tail. I cast an eye in Becky's direction. She was already lowering the saddle onto Charlie's back.

Standing by Honey's near shoulder, I hoisted the saddle up, settling it lightly onto her back, then tugged the saddle blanket back gently so that her coat wouldn't get caught underneath it and rub. I power-walked to her offside, making sure the saddlecloth was flat, and let down the girth.

'Yes!'

I looked up. Becky had just done up her last girth point and emerged the clear winner.

'How'd you do that?'

Becky laughed. 'Magic.'

I returned to Honey's nearside and reached out for the girth, fastening it. I patted Honey's side and let down my stirrup.

'Ready to go?'

I looked over my shoulder. Becky was mounted. Charlie tossed his head, impatient to get going. I checked my girth, managing to tighten it two more notches, then picked up each of Honey's front feet, one at a time, and pulled them towards me for a moment, giving her forelegs a good stretch.

'As loser of the saddle-up challenge it's your duty to open and close the corral gate,' Becky said.

I groaned and held my reins just under Honey's chin with my right hand and at the buckle with my left. 'Naturally. Would you like me to peel you a grape while I'm at it?'

Becky thought about this for a second. 'Yes. And I wouldn't mind a cheese and peanut butter sandwich.'

I led Honey to the gate and pulled a face. 'That's totally disgusting.'

'You don't know what you're missing out on, Ash!' Becky cried, walking Charlie through the gate.

31

'I don't wanna know what I'm missing out on,' I said, closing the gate behind the four of us. It was time to mount. Once my left foot was in the stirrup it took one bounce and I was settling myself into the saddle. At last. The place I most wanted to be.

'It'll take us about twenty minutes to get there,' Becky said once we got moving. 'That's a pretty good warm-up.'

'Say the word "warm" some more,' I grumbled, shrinking into my jacket. 'Maybe if you keep saying it I might start feeling it.'

Becky laughed and urged Charlie into a relaxed trot. Honey followed suit at the slightest touch of my heels.

'Looking forward to meeting the McMurray girls?' Becky asked.

'Totally,' I said. 'They sound awesome.'

Becky raised her eyebrows.

'What?' I cried.

'Nothing,' Becky said. We trotted our horses past Shady Creek Primary School. I laughed, despite myself. How cool, how totally completely cool was it to be riding past my school on my horse! I missed my old life sometimes. I missed Jenna and my old school in the city. But Shady Creek was my home now. Honey and Becky had made it my home. And I never ever wanted to leave.

'It's just that you're not always the best judge of character.'

I brought Honey to a halt.

'What are you talking about?' I said. 'When haven't I been a good judge of character?'

Becky pulled Charlie up and turned to look at me, surprised. She scratched her chin and stared at the sky for a moment. 'Let's see. There's your first day in Shady Creek when you trusted Flea and let him talk you into riding that maniac horse of his. And there's being totally tricked by Carly's cousin at Waratah Grove and there's—'

I urged Honey into a walk again. 'Enough! This time'll be different. Mrs Mac is nuts about them and that's good enough for me.'

Becky shrugged. 'Okay. Just keep your eyes open.'

Becky rode ahead of me. I glowered at her back. She's my best friend and I'm crazy about her, but sometimes she makes me mad. It's not that she's trying to be mean or anything. Becky would never do that. It's just that sometimes she says exactly what I'm thinking but am too afraid to admit to her, or even to myself.

Becky and I followed the trail through the bush to the long dirt road. So much had happened between us since I'd arrived in Shady Creek not even a year ago. We'd met at Riding Club and become best friends. We'd found Honey together and rescued her. But then things became tense between Becky and me when Jenna had come to stay, and I felt bad when Becky broke her arm and I competed in the Waratah Grove Junior Cross-Country Riding Championships in her place and won. Our friendship was really put to the test when Mrs Mac bought the run-down farm and transformed it into Shady Trails Riding Ranch, a horse-lover's paradise. Becky hadn't been too pleased about Shady Trails at first. She'd worried that Riding Club couldn't compete and she'd even refused to speak to me once she'd found out I was working there. But everything worked out fine. Becky and I are still best friends.

'Here we are!' Becky sang.

I shook my head. I'd been so caught up in my thoughts that I'd barely noticed our arrival.

'Wow and wow,' I sighed. No matter how many times I'd been to Shady Trails, no matter how many times I'd go in the future, the Ranch never failed to take my breath away. I could still barely believe that the place where my gorgeous Honey horse had almost died had become this lush, green haven for horses, where horse crazy kids like Becky, our amazing friend Priyanka Prasad (Pree, or Preezy-Boo, Preety-Bops or Preencess), who was always telling horsy jokes, and me could ride, learn, work and play.

'You can say that again,' Becky said. It had taken her a while to come around to the whole Trails experience, but once she'd had her first taste she was a committed Trailer.

'Wow and wow,' I giggled.

'I didn't mean literally.' Becky rolled her eyes as she turned Charlie into the Shady Trails entrance and through the grand archway. He didn't need a lot of encouragement. Both he and Honey were practically dancing on their forelegs with excitement.

'Well, this is it,' I said, almost to myself. 'Ready or not, McMurray girls. Here we come.'

four

Face to Face

My tummy was fizzy, just like it is before a show. Or a Maths test.

Becky and I trotted our horses all the way down the driveway. Past the paddocks where a few school and about a dozen agisted horses grazed contentedly. I'd be feeding them soon. All the horses were handfed twice a day, no matter the state of the grass. They were working horses and needed fuel.

Sitting up tall on my Honey's back I could see the round yards, the holding yard and the arena. Straight ahead was the Shady Trails complex, an amazing horseshoe-shaped building boasting a reception area for riders, a café, a party room (where I vowed most solemnly that I would be having my twelfth birthday party), washrooms and a gear and souvenir shop. It was wrapped around the holding yard giving riders, party-goers, shoppers and parents the chance to watch the comings and goings of the horses. The bush trails and more paddocks stretched out behind the complex.

We pulled up just outside the office and had barely dismounted before Mrs McMurray appeared. She looked different. Like someone had reached into her heart and flicked a switch. She was all lit up.

'Ash, love! And Becky, thank goodness. I'm so glad you're here.' Mrs Mac waved her hands at her lips, like she had something really hot in her mouth. Her blue eyes were shining.

'How are you, Mrs McMurray?' I asked, sliding to the ground. I held Honey's reins under her chin and stroked her face.

Mrs Mac clapped like a little kid with a whole box of chocolates to herself. 'They're here. They're really here!'

Becky and I exchanged glances. Mrs Mac's eyebrows were raised so high they'd nearly disappeared.

'That's great,' I said, rubbing gently under Honey's chin. She nibbled on my hand. 'Isn't it, Beck?'

'Great!' she said.

I felt better about meeting them. Anyone who could do this to Mrs Mac must be all right. I just hoped they loved horses. It would be okay with me if they didn't. I mean, Jenna's my best friend in the world, along with Becky, and she couldn't tell a stock saddle from an all-purpose saddle for all the bytes in cyberspace. But then again, I wouldn't know a byte if it came up and bit me. Being best friends has never meant we've had to be the same. But I have to admit it. I do love the fact that Becky is as totally horse mad as I am.

'C'mon and meet them, you two.' Mrs McMurray beamed at us. 'They're in the office. They're dying to get to know you and I promised them you'd show them all around Shady Trails on horseback.'

I nodded, so did Becky, and we looped our free arms together.

'Girls!' Mrs McMurray called in the direction of the office. 'Oh, Ash, love, I'm so glad you're going to be looking after them. What with running the Ranch and everything I ... Girls! And you, Becky, know all the best trails and places to go in Shady ... *Girls!*'

The door of the office opened and a tall, thin girl with long blonde hair stepped outside. I was shocked to see her wearing a short-sleeved shirt and a skirt so tiny it looked like it needed nourishment. I looked down at my own grubby joddies, dusty chapettes and thick winter coat.

Tall-and-Blonde was followed by a shorter, dark-haired girl dressed in thick pants, boots and a long woollen overcoat. Her eyes were darting all over the place and terror was etched on her pale face. She seemed to be doing some sort of sword-fighting dance, but as she got closer I realized she was whipping at the air with a black riding crop.

'There are so many flies here, Nanna,' she cried, making an ear-splitting *whoosh* sound with her crop. I smiled to myself, loving the sound of her English accent. It wasn't something any Creeker heard too often. 'Mother would not be at all pleased if I contracted a fly-borne disease. She told me I must phone her *immediately* if I was ever exposed to disease.'

Mrs Mac beamed and stroked the girl's shoulder-length hair. 'Mikenzie, love, this is Ashleigh. Ash is one of my—'

'I feel a chill in the air, Nanna. Mother said I must phone her *immediately* if I was ever exposed to extreme weather conditions.' Mikenzie frowned at Mrs Mac and drew her overcoat close to her. 'The cold and flies cannot be good for my health. Mother assured me before we left England that the delicacy of my constitution had been made quite plain to you.'

Mrs McMurray laughed. 'Oh, Mickie! Isn't that the cutest thing you ever heard?'

I elbowed Becky whose mouth had dropped open.

'Careful, Beck,' I hissed. 'You're exposing your tonsils to extreme weather and flies.'

'There are no flies,' she said through a fake smile. 'The kid's seeing—'

Tall-and-Blonde, who had Mrs Mac's blue eyes, had been looking us both up and down as though we were horses she was considering buying. I wondered if I should let her check my teeth or lift my feet. Once inspection was complete she raised her chin and watched us through her eyelashes. When she finally spoke, she sounded very bored. 'Are these the stablehands?'

'Ash, Becky,' Mrs McMurray said, tugging on Tall-and-Blonde's hand. 'I'd be delighted to introduce you to my eldest granddaughter, Savannah. Savvy's twelve, aren't you, love?'

Savannah shrugged and looked over our heads. 'Yes,' she said, sounding as though she'd rather be anywhere else in the world than here. 'I suppose that makes me the oldest one here. Neither of you looks twelve.'

'I'm twelve,' Becky said, folding her arms. 'I turned twelve two months ago.'

Savannah beamed. 'Ha! I'm the oldest, just like I said. I turned twelve three months ago.' There was a sudden sparkle in her voice, like she had something to be excited about at last.

I nudged Becky as discreetly as I could.

Mrs Mac clapped her hands like an excited little girl. 'I'll leave you girls to get to know one another. Have fun, you four!'

With that she disappeared. Becky, Savannah, Mikenzie and I stared at each other for a few moments. A few long, awkward moments.

I looked at Becky. Becky looked back at me. I looked at the McMurray girls. Savannah was inspecting her long pink fingernails and Mikenzie was frantically swatting at the air, the collar of her overcoat now pulled over her nose and mouth.

I cleared my throat. 'So, uh, can we, uh, call you guys Savvy and Mickie or—'

Savannah's eyes flashed. 'Absolutely not! Mother detests those nicknames and has told our father many times that he's to stop Nanna from using them.'

Becky gasped, her eyes so wide I thought she was having a fit. Her arm tightened around mine.

'D'you, uh, d'you wanna go for a ride or something?' I said, trying to be as friendly as I could.

Mikenzie shook her head and waved her crop back and forth across her face like a windscreen wiper. 'Mother said I'm not to go anywhere near the animals. I might be allergic. She said I might be trampled or even bitten. Mother told Nanna that I wasn't to be exposed to trampling.'

'How 'bout you?' I said, indicating Savannah.

'That's what I'm here to do, isn't it? I need to get straight into training. Nanna told me there's a show on soon and I'll be entering, of course. There's nothing left for me to do but compete overseas — I won everything there was to win at home.'

'You did?' I stared at her, my eyes so wide they were beginning to ache.

'Of course,' Savannah declared. 'I almost made it to the Nationals. Have either of you two ever almost made it to the Nationals?'

'Not—' Becky began.

'Ha!' Savannah cried, bouncing on her toes. 'I knew I'd be the best rider here. I only wish I could've brought my horse, Golden Dream. He's a Palomino. I won High Point Junior Youth last year. Have either of you two ever won High Point Junior Youth?'

'We-uh—' I stammered.

'Ha!' Savannah clapped her hands. 'I knew it. I knew I'd be the only High Pointer here. This is so cool!'

'About the ride,' I said, trying to squash what felt very much like the onset of hyperventilation. I held tighter to Becky's arm and gave her a look. Her expression had changed from one of shock to one of total annoyance.

'Oh yes, yes,' Savannah said, flicking her fingers at us. 'I'm sure you understand by now that I'm an excellent rider. I will be requiring an excellent mount.'

My mouth dropped open. Becky stifled a gag.

'Your wish is our command,' Becky said, slightly recovered. A huge grin was splashed across her face.

Savannah lifted her chin and smiled. 'I'm going to change. I only have the best riding clothes. I refuse to wear anything but Eurochampion. I don't suppose you're wearing Eurochampion?'

I shook my head. 'Planet Horse, in town.'

'Ha! I knew I'd be the only one here with genuine Eurochampion gear. I'll bet you've never even seen Eurochampion up close!'

Becky and I shook our heads.

'Ha!' Savannah grinned and raised her chin even higher and put her hands on her hips. Her long blonde hair flapped against her back like a cape. I scrutinized her, waiting for her to leap a tall stable or be more powerful than a Clydie–Shire cross.

She turned and marched in the direction of Mrs McMurray's place, her long blonde hair swishing from side to side. Mikenzie tripped after her, clutching her coat tightly around her neck.

'Can you believe them?' I said once they were out of earshot. 'I think Mrs Mac picked up the wrong kids from the airport. These two can't have a single drop of McMurray blood in them.'

'So now do you believe me?' Becky asked, wearing a look of complete satisfaction.

'What about?' I rubbed Honey's face and planted a kiss on her nose.

'That you're a terrible judge of character.' Becky lifted Charlie's saddle flap and loosened his girth. 'He needs a breather.'

I followed suit, letting Honey's girth down a few notches. 'If I'm such a bad judge of character why are we best friends?'

Becky laughed. 'Who knows? Maybe I am as well!'

'Funny.'

We led the horses up and down the driveway, keeping them warm as we waited for Savannah.

The minutes ticked by slowly, until finally an hour had passed.

'Where is she?' Becky wailed. 'This is not good for my horse. Or yours, for that matter.'

'I'm gonna stable her,' I said, sighing sharply. 'What about you?'

Becky's face was red. 'I can't hang around any longer. Dad made me promise to work today. With Rachael out here all the time, he needs me for the lunch rush. Charlie'll need to be cooled out, groomed and fed as well!'

'Go,' I said. 'I can handle her. Besides, maybe you should just ask your dad about this Western stuff. It's better than worrying about it.'

Becky tightened her girth and stretched Charlie's legs. 'I dunno, Ash.'

'What don't you know?'

Becky sighed. 'Dad taught me everything I know about horses. He taught me to ride. Why didn't he tell me about this? What if I do ask him and he gets mad?'

I made a small shrug, not knowing what to say.

'It's obvious,' Becky said, swinging into her saddle. 'He doesn't want me to know.'

'Maybe he's got a good reason.' I couldn't think of a reason why Gary would hide his past Western life from Becky, but I knew something for sure. If Gary was my dad, I'd be just as confused as Becky was.

It was Becky's turn to shrug. 'Who knows? Will you be all right with Savannah on your own?'

I nodded. 'No worries. Go home. I'll be fine. I mean, how much trouble can she be?'

five

The Shady Boa

'Where's your friend?' Savannah McMurray looked around the stables. She was dressed from head to foot in nothing but the finest Eurochampion riding clothes. Her black leather boots shone. Her helmet was covered in rich navy-blue velvet. Her cream joddies looked fresh enough to eat. She was wearing a white long-sleeved shirt with the word *Eurochampion* embroidered across the collar in neat gold letters, and a gorgeous navy-blue waistcoat with gold buttons. Something inside me tingled.

'She had to go,' I said. 'What took you so long?'

Savannah arched one sleek eyebrow. 'Looking this good doesn't come quick or cheap.'

'Is this safe?' Mikenzie cautiously tiptoed into the

stable. She spun in a slow circle, surveying the entire stable complex as though it would swallow her up at any second.

'Thought you weren't riding,' I said. 'Thought you weren't to be exposed to trampling.'

Mikenzie's eyes widened. 'Nana rang Mother and promised her that you'd take care of me.'

Savannah took a step towards me and fixed her blue eyes on mine. 'Yeah.'

I wished instantly for Becky to come back.

'I'll tack up a quiet little pony for you,' I said. 'He's very clean so it's okay to take off the mask.'

Mikenzie shook her head and pressed the surgical mask she was wearing tight over her nose and mouth.

'It's really not a good idea to ride like that,' I said. 'Especially with those rubber gloves on.'

Mikenzie looked at her hands, which were sporting thin white-coloured gloves, the kind a dentist wears when they're digging around in your mouth. Unless Mikenzie was planning to inspect her horse's teeth, I didn't see much point in her wearing them.

'They're latex,' Mikenzie declared. 'Anyway, it's not possible. I simply must protect myself from infection.'

I smiled. 'Have it your way. But you'll sweat in those things. Isn't sweat germy?'

Mikenzie's face went all pasty under her mask. I smiled again, this time on the inside.

I led Penelope over to Savannah. The sweet chestnut mare with the extra thick mane and the long white blaze on her face, almost identical to Honey's, reached out to Savannah with her soft white nose as if to say, 'Hi, wanna go for a ride?'

'Is this what you call your best horse? I told you, I'm an excellent rider. This is nothing but a school pony.' Savannah stood with her hands on her hips.

'Penny's a registered Hanoverian,' I said, stung. 'She's one of our most amazing horses. Well, I mean, they're all amazing, but she's very special. She was an eventer before she came here.'

Savannah's eyes lit up. 'Is she the *only* Hanoverian here?'

I nodded. 'She's the only one in Shady Creek.'

'Ha!' Savannah clapped her hands. '*I* get to ride the only Hanoverian. While I'm here *I'm* the only one who's allowed to ride her, okay?'

I bit my lip. 'She's used for training by riders learning eventing. She's booked out all the time.'

Savannah snatched her reins from my hand. 'Not while I'm here. And if I find out any other rider has even looked at her I'll tell Nanna. Promise me I'll be her only rider.'

'I-I can't.' Surely Savannah could understand that she was asking the impossible. How could I control who rode Penelope when I was at school all week? Mikenzie wasn't even paying attention. She was holding her mask over her nose and mouth with one gloved hand and madly swatting at non-existent flies with the other. 'Anyway, it's up to your Nan. This is her place, not mine.'

Savannah mounted right there in the stables.

'No one's allowed to ride in the stables,' I said. 'Ranch rules.'

'Those rules don't apply to me,' Savannah said, looking down at me from Penelope's back. 'I'm a McMurray. This is McMurray property, remember?'

'Where's my horse?' Mikenzie's voice was muffled.

'Take off that stupid thing,' Savannah said, patting Penny's sleek golden neck. 'Nobody can understand a word you're saying.'

I rubbed my forehead with my fingertips. 'I'll get him.'

Bartok was a cute grey pony who could be won over for life with a slice of carrot. I tacked him up and led him from his stall and out into the doorway of the stables where Mikenzie was waiting.

'Is it clean? Is it sterile?'

'He's a he, not an it, and yes, he's clean.' I held out the reins to Mikenzie.

'But is it *sterile*?' Mikenzie insisted from behind her surgical mask, her eyes serious.

I had a quick think. Bartok is a gelding, which, technically, makes him sterile.

'Yes.' I nodded. 'Most definitely, yes.'

Mikenzie's hand fluttered against her chest. She sighed and took Bartok's reins.

'I'll get my horse,' I muttered, contemplating changing my name and moving to Timbuktu. I only hoped Timbuktu was horse friendly.

I led Honey from her stall, her stirrups shortened so they wouldn't knock into her sides.

'That's *your* horse?' Savannah said, incredulous. Her eyes were wide and she had the kind of smile on her face that always preceded a ...

'Ha!' she said. 'You've got a part-breed. What on earth is it? It looks like it was left on someone's doorstep in a basket.'

My insides boiled. 'Her name is Honey and she's a champion.'

'Ha!' Savannah laughed. 'The horse I ride back home is a real champion. He won Champion Arabian Stallion this year.'

'Whatever,' I grumbled, biting my tongue so hard I didn't know if I'd ever speak again. Carly and the Creeps serving it up to me was one thing. I'd come to accept it was just part of living in Shady Creek. But having it dumped on me from Mrs Mac's granddaughter was something else. I wanted, needed this job. I loved Shady Trails and Mrs Mac had become a friend, as well as my boss. The money I earned was also keeping Honey in horseshoes.

I led Honey from the stable and looked up at the sky, hoping, praying for rain. Or a blizzard. Anything! But the sky was a clear blue.

'Well, are we riding?' Savannah chirped.

I lifted my saddle flap and tightened my girth then gave Honey's legs a stretch. I lengthened my stirrups and gathered my reins at the base of her neck, careful not to yank on her mouth. In less than thirty seconds I was in the saddle.

'Ooh, look!' Savannah said, grinning. 'I'm higher

than you. Penelope must be at least a hand taller than your horse.'

Savannah clapped her hands like she'd just won first prize. I shook my head. This wasn't what riding was about. Not for me, anyway.

'Ooh, ooh!' Mikenzie wailed from Bartok's saddle.

'What is it now?' Savannah snapped.

Mikenzie pointed at Honey, an expression of horror etched on her face. 'That horse made a smell!'

'That's what horses do,' I said.

'Ha! I never smelled it,' Savannah said, grinning. 'Just you. Ha!'

'Let's go this way,' I sighed. I pushed Honey past Penny and rode her out of the holding yard and towards the path that led on to the trails, not really caring if my two new best friends were coming or not.

It wasn't until Honey and I were well down the one-hour trail (there was no way I was going riding with them for even a minute longer!) that I even looked over my shoulder to check that the McMurray girls were there.

Savannah pointed at a fork in the trail. 'Let's go this way.'

'No,' I said. 'Stick to this trail.'

'This trail's boring. It's all just trees and rocks.' Savannah pulled Penny's head towards the fork.

'No!' I said again. 'We could get lost. There are hundreds of acres of bush trails here. Your Nan's told us over and over to stick to the marked trails.'

'Ha!' Savannah cried. 'You're scared. Ha!'

Mikenzie whimpered, 'I wanna go home. I wanna go home.'

Savannah kicked Penny hard behind her girth. 'I'm going. You babies can come with me or stay here and cry.'

'You can't!' I howled, imagining the trouble I'd be in if I returned to the stables with one less McMurray.

'Why not?' Savannah said, a haughty look on her face.

It was my turn to grin. 'Snakes. Lots of snakes. Red-bellies and browns. We've got the deadliest snakes in the world out here in Shady Creek. If a snake bites you, you're dead before you even have a chance to scream.'

Okay, so I was exaggerating ever so slightly. All right, I was exaggerating a lot. But the whole morning was really beginning to get to me. In fact, I was over it. I was over the McMurrays and I wasn't even halfway through the first day. I wished then and there that when I'd promised Mrs Mac I'd look after her precious girls during their stay in Shady Creek that I'd crossed my fingers behind my back.

'S–snakes?' Mikenzie stammered. 'R–real snakes? Poisonous s–snakes?'

I nodded slowly. 'Yep. And that's not all. Shady Creek is known all over the world for the Shady Boa.'

Savannah narrowed her eyes and regarded me. 'Shady Boa? I've never heard of it.'

'That's because no one who's seen a Shady Boa has ever lived to tell the tale.' I lowered my voice to a whisper and looked over my shoulder. 'But I know this for sure. A Shady Boa will eat a horse and rider in one bite, tack and all. They especially love grey ponies.'

Mikenzie screamed — the longest, loudest scream I'd ever heard.

She turned, kicked poor Bartok hard behind his girth and trotted for her life back down the trail towards the complex.

Savannah looked at me, her head to one side. 'Is there really a Shady Boa?'

'Course there is,' I said, winding a strip of Honey's copper-coloured mane around my forefinger. 'Ask any Creeker. They'll tell you.'

Savannah was silent. Then she turned Penelope to follow Mikenzie, leaving me alone with Honey. By the time I'd gathered my thoughts and my reins and followed Savannah back towards the Ranch, the McMurrays were out of sight. They were nowhere to be seen in the yards, the stables or anywhere else. I knew I had to take care of Penny and Bartok, who'd been dumped in the holding yard. First I stabled and untacked Honey, throwing a light rug over her while she dried out, then led Penny and Bartok to their stalls.

'She didn't even loosen your girth,' I muttered, furious, as I lifted Penny's saddle flap. 'That's the least she could have done.'

I gave the horses a quick brush each and turned them out into the front paddock where all the Ranch horses were kept during the day. Then I went in search of Pree and Sam and, avoiding saying a single word about the trail ride, took two pony leads, mucked out five stalls and climbed up on the tractor behind Azz to toss the afternoon feed of lucerne hay to the school horses.

At the end of the day I mounted my Honey horse once more and rode down the long Trails driveway towards the gate.

'Thanks for today!' a voice called from behind me.

I twisted around in the saddle. Savannah was standing outside the office in her miniskirt and sandals, her arms folded across her chest.

'You're welcome!' I called back.

'We learned a lot about Shady Creek. And the kind of people who live here.' Savannah smiled, a quick, plastic smile, and disappeared inside Mrs Mac's office.

I clucked my tongue and pressed my heels to Honey's sides, my head reeling. What did Savannah want with me? What had she said to Mrs Mac? Had she said anything at all? I couldn't be sure. But one thing I did know was that Savannah McMurray had power. And although I'd only known her for a day, I was convinced that she would use it to get anything she wanted.

'How'd it go?' Mum looked up briefly from her colour charts. They were spread all over the kitchen table. I looked at the clock.

'We're having cereal for dinner again, aren't we?'

'That's not answering my question.' Mum raised her eyebrows at me. I knew there was no way out.

'It was …' I began. I slopped into a chair and stretched out my legs, knocking my boots together. 'Different.'

'Is that all?' Mum folded her arms. 'You couldn't wait to meet them. All I've heard was the McMurray girls this, that and three bags full for weeks. And now that you finally get to spend a whole day with them you have nothing to say.'

I felt all yucky, like the last thing in the world I wanted to do was talk, much less about those girls. 'Why are you so interested?'

Mum frowned. 'First, that was cheeky, Miss. Secondly, Mrs McMurray just called. We had an interesting chat.'

I sat up instantly, my boots slapping onto the kitchen floor. Mum grimaced at the sight of clods of grass, mud and possibly horse poo skittling across the tiles. 'What about?'

Mum sighed. 'She wasn't happy. She said you ruined Susannah's first day at Shady Trails.'

My heart thumped. 'It's Savannah. And how did I ruin *her* day?'

Mum rubbed her forehead with her fingertips. 'She said her granddaughters are very upset. She said you told them that there are man-eating snakes roaming the streets of Shady Creek. Now they're too afraid to go outside. I'm so disappointed, Ash.'

'I never said man-eating!' I cried.

Mum frowned. Her lips were thin. 'What did you say?'

I stared at the tablecloth. I'd never realized just how interesting the pattern was before. Grapes and flowers. Nice.

'Ashleigh Louise Miller!'

I sighed and held up my hands. If she'd typed up a confession and handed me a pen I'd have signed it. 'I told them there were horse-and-rider eating snakes. But I never said anything about roaming the streets.'

'You need to ring Mrs McMurray and apologize,' Mum said, her cheeks flushing. 'I just can't believe you'd say something like that to two girls on an overseas holiday. Don't you remember being new to Shady Creek?'

'Only too well.' I folded my arms, so mad my head was throbbing.

'Ring now and apologize.'

I stood up. 'But, Mum!'

Mum stood as well. 'But, Mum, nothing. Apologize or you're grounded!'

My mouth dropped open. 'That's so unfair! You should've heard what they were saying to me. I gave them the best horses, but nothing was good enough for them. Nothing.'

Mum pointed at the phone. I shook my head.

'Don't make me count to three, young lady.'

I pushed past my mother and headed towards the back door. 'I've got jobs to do.'

'If you take one step out of the house you are grounded!' Mum yelled.

I opened the back door and turned to look at her. Hot tears pricked at my eyes. 'Fine.'

I ran into the semi-darkness, slamming the door as hard as I could behind me.

'Trouble in paradise, Spiller?' came a voice from behind the fence.

'Drop dead, Fleabag!' I shrieked. He had a gift, that was for sure. He always caught me at my worst. I knew that by Monday morning everyone at school would have heard all about my troubles.

I ran to the paddock and wriggled under the fence, calling out to Honey. She looked up at me from under her tree where she was eating her dinner of white and green chaff and horse pellets. Toffee was huddled close by her side.

Honey nickered to me and I wrapped my arms around her neck, sobbing into her winter rug. It was so unfair.

I slid to the ground and leaned up against the tree. Once I'd had a good cry (and mumbled a whole lot of things about Savannah, Mikenzie, Mrs McMurray and Mum that I really didn't mean), I felt better.

Toffee had finished his dinner. The mini picked up his soccer ball with his teeth and threw it into my lap with one toss of his head.

'Wanna play?' I said, wiping my nose on my jacket sleeve, just to annoy Mum.

Toffee whinnied and tossed his head again. He looked so funny with his winter coat — all fuzzy-wuzzy and warm.

I scrambled to my feet and ran across the paddock with the ball. Toffee followed me, pig-rooting and grunting with delight. I dropped the ball and kicked it. Toffee galloped past me and skidded over the ball, snatching it up in his mouth. He stopped dead and tossed it high in the air. I ran, jumped and made the catch, then kicked it as hard as I could. He chased the ball, bouncing across the paddock like a very hairy, vertically challenged gazelle.

Finally I begged Toff for mercy. After a full day at Shady Trails, a fight with Mum and a cry worthy of an Academy Award, I was wiped out. I lay on the grass watching the sunset.

The sun was now almost completely gone and it was dark in the paddock. I shivered and shrank deeper into my jacket. My stomach growled and I headed for home, intending to cut myself a huge slice of humble pie for dinner.

six

Western Pleasure

'Who can name the main Western horse breeds?' Gary stood on his milk crate, watching the Shady Creek riders. We were mounted, inspected, warmed-up and ready for anything.

'Quarter Horse, Appaloosa, Palouse Pony and Paint!' Flea cried.

'What are you doing?' Carly hissed, her face twisted. Destiny tossed her head and Carly slapped the mare's white neck.

Flea gave her a blank look and shrugged. He loved Western riding and seemed thrilled it had finally become part of Riding Club. At least now he wasn't saying anything laced with spite.

'Right!' Gary beamed. 'It's great you guys are so keen to learn Western. It's one of Australia's most popular horse sports and the Pinebark Ridge Western Riding Club Show is just the tip of the haystack.'

'Don't you mean tip of the iceberg?' Carly curled her lip.

'We're not in Antarctica,' Jodie snapped.

'Why would anyone want to learn Western anyway? It's not even proper riding.' Trust Carly.

'That's not true,' Flea said, his face flushing. He squeezed his reins tight. 'I just joined Pinebark Ridge Western Riding Club. They get heaps of new members every month. Isn't that right, Scud?'

Flea dropped his hand to his gelding's neck. The horse stood tall and proud, almost daring anybody to challenge his master.

'Some people take it up because they feel so secure in the Western saddle, with its large horn in front and deep seat, and let's not forget that a properly trained Western horse will stop when the rider says, "Whoa",' Gary said. 'Others love the thrill of the rodeo.'

'What kind of idiot would want to get bucked off a horse? On purpose!' Carly bawled.

'Put a sock in it, will ya?' Flea growled.

Carly's mouth dropped open and her cheeks reddened. Flea glared straight ahead. Ryan gazed at the sky. Becky and I exchanged amazed glances.

'Bronc riding, or riding an unbroken horse, is only one part of the rodeo. There's also cutting, where a rider chooses a calf to separate from a herd of cattle and has to allow their horse to get on with the job. There's steer wrestling and—'

'Okay, okay,' Carly said in a sour voice. 'I get the picture.'

'Terrific,' Gary said. 'Now it's time to ride! Stay in your straight line. We'll be riding off one at a time. Flea, once again you're our demo man for the day.'

Flea beamed. I'd never seen him beam before. I'd seen him sneer, smirk, scowl and snarl. But never a beam. Something was happening to him. It was creepy. Fascinating, but creepy.

Flea moved Scud out of the line and walked towards Gary. He murmured a barely audible 'Whoa', and Scud halted beside Gary. I was amazed to see Scud stop dead in his tracks at the slightest command from Flea. I couldn't believe I'd never noticed it before. But then again, I'd never wanted to look all that closely at the horse and his rider, Shady Creek's King Creep.

'Flea's going to demonstrate the Western walk for you today, then two new gaits. The jog and the lope.' Gary patted Scud's rump. Flea tipped his helmet and Scud walked into the arena.

'How did he do that?' Jodie cried. 'Flea didn't move his leg!'

'The Western horse is trained to respond to the slightest signal,' Gary explained. His eyes followed Flea around the arena. So did mine. Scud's head was so low that the tips of his ears and the top of his withers were level. Flea sat up straight with a deep seat and a long leg. He held his reins in his right hand and looked ahead.

'I've asked Flea to wear his spurs today, which at an ordinary Riding Club meeting would be banned,' Gary continued. 'But in Western riding, spurs are permissible. The Western rider uses the spurs, rather than a kick of the leg, plus the weight of the reins and his or her seat to cue the horse.'

Scud turned the corner without Flea putting pressure on his inside rein.

'Now what happened?' Julie asked. 'It's like he's just sitting there and Scud knows just what to do.'

'Simple,' Gary said. 'Scud is trained to steer around in response to Flea's leg pressure. If Flea uses his outside leg, Scud will turn to the left. If Flea uses his inside leg Scud will turn to the right. Scud is moving away from the pressure. It's a pretty remarkable partnership.'

'Dressage,' I murmured. 'It's just like dressage.'

'Hmm.' I could tell Becky was thinking really hard. So was I. About Western, about Flea. It was all so new, but so amazing. I wanted to try it. I had to try it.

'Jog him now for me, will you, mate?' Gary called. Flea gave a small nod of his head and made a clucking noise with his tongue. Scud responded with a slow, collected-style trot. Flea's seat never left the saddle. He sat deep, and relaxed. I felt a flicker of envy. I'd never believed Flea to be any more than a huge pain in my backside. And my backyard!

Now here he was demonstrating this wonderful relationship with his horse, the kind that I wanted with Honey. She usually did whatever I asked her to, no *problemo*. But she'd never responded to a voice command.

'The jog, you should have noticed, is basically an English trot that is a bit slower than usual. It's a natural gait and is easy on the horse's joints.' Gary folded his arms and smiled warmly at Flea. 'Notice that Scud's hindquarters are doing most of the work.

All the impulsion, all the drive, the moving forward is coming from those back legs. They're the engine pushing him forward. A lope now, mate!'

Flea made another noise that sounded suspiciously like he was blowing a raspberry. Scud moved immediately into an easy canter.

'Did he just *raspberry*?' I said, stunned.

'No, he kissed.' Gary nodded.

The Shady Creek riders giggled.

'It's true. A Western horse is trained to lope with the rider's legs on him and a kiss noise. Remember, the lope is the Western canter.'

'Cool!' I had to do this. If Flea could do it, I could do it. I wanted to start training and I wanted to start now.

Later that day, every Shady Creek rider from Under 10s to Opens sat mounted on their horses, side by side, in a single line. Gary sat mounted on Bonnie. Since I'd joined Riding Club, I'd only ever seen him ride her a few times during lessons.

'First of all we're going to make sure our seats are perfect! We should all be sitting vertically, like I showed you last time, with a straight back. No slumping! Carly you look like an "S".'

'You look like an "L",' Carly muttered under her breath. 'As in *Loser*.'

'Shoulders, hip and heel should all align, same as the English seat. Now for the Western difference. Remember that a Western rider sits deep, like a dressage rider.'

'I can do that!' I cried. All the other riders laughed.

'We don't all have Western or dressage saddles so some of you may need to lower your stirrups a notch or two. The lower leg position should automatically deepen your seat.'

There was a flurry of stirrup leather loosening, mine included. Gary was right. I did feel like I had a deeper seat.

'Legs bent slightly at the knee. All your weight in your heels. Tuck your seats under. Shoulders back. Eyes ahead. Now to make cowboys and cowgirls out of you. Take both reins in one hand. Perfect!'

I had a quick look up and down the line of riders. I'd never seen them this keen about anything before. All we needed were ten-gallon hats.

'Flea, would you like to take over and show everyone how to drop their horse's head?' Gary said, sitting deep and relaxed in his saddle. He had assumed a Western seat and was holding both reins in his right hand above the horn. His left hand hung by his side, just as it had in some of those old photos.

'Me? Teach the class?' Flea was gobsmacked.

Gary nodded. 'Why not?'

Becky cleared her throat loudly. I cast her a sideways glance.

'What's Dad doing?' she hissed. 'He knows more about Western than Fleabag ever will.'

I leaned across in my saddle and patted her knee, then turned to stare at Flea.

Flea made another of those barely perceptible squeezes of his leg against Scud's side and the black gelding moved from the line. Flea turned and faced us, grinning from ear to ear, like he'd been waiting his whole life for this moment.

'You have to learn to ask your horses to drop their heads, to hold them down low in the natural Western position. None of that arched neck stuff. Hold your horse's barrel with both legs and jiggle your reins.' Flea held his chin up. 'Not all the horses here'll respond. There are only a few with any real Western training, and it does take a while for them to learn. But all of you should try.'

I did as I was told, holding my calf muscles against Honey's belly and jiggling my reins. Nothing.

'If you get their heads down take the pressure off the reins. Always take away the pressure when the horse is doing what you want. But hold 'em up — keep your legs on 'em.'

I kept jiggling my reins, but still nothing. I looked up and down the line. Becky kicked at my foot and urged me to look at her father. Bonnie had responded just like Flea had said. There was no denying it. Gary knew what he was doing.

'Hold your reins in your right hand or left hand — whatever's comfortable for you. There's only one rule — the slack of your reins must fall on the same side of the horse's neck as the hand you're holding them with. Got that?'

We nodded and Flea demonstrated for us. He looked really cool sitting in his very own black Western saddle on a coal-black horse. 'Your hand should be just above the horn. If you don't have a Western saddle, imagine there's a horn. Then drop your free hand straight down.'

We did as we were told. I would never normally do anything Flea said, but he knew what he was talking about when it came to Western riding. If

Gary wasn't going to open up about his past, Flea was our only hope of ribbons in the Western Show.

'Put your inside legs on 'em, just behind the girth. Now squeeze more. That should make 'em turn right,' Flea said, demonstrating a turn.

'Good job, Flea. I want you all to walk in a circle now and practise holding your hands correctly, staying relaxed in the saddle and using your seats,' Gary called.

We all turned single file and rode into the arena one after the other. I held my reins in my right hand and let my left hand drop. My legs were long and my seat was deep. Honey moved steadily and, while the chances of her dancing the two-step were higher than the chances of her dropping her head, I felt like a Western rider for the first time. And it was all thanks to Flea!

We walked around the arena in both directions practising a Western walk, but by the end of the lesson none of us (except Flea, Gary and maybe a girl in the Opens) had come even close to a Western walk with a dropped head. Still, we'd had a great time trying.

'Didja see Dad?' Becky hissed as we cooled Charlie and Honey out, walking them in circles.

'I can't believe him. Does he think I'm stupid? He can't expect me to believe that he knows nothing about Western. Not after today.'

I shrugged. I didn't know what to say to her. What do you say to your best friend when they find out their dad has been keeping a secret from them for their whole life?

I snuck a peek at Gary who had dismounted and was speaking intently with Flea in the arena. I looked at Becky. Once I saw the hurt and confusion in her eyes I knew I had to help her.

seven

Western Rookie

'How many posters do you need, exactly?' Becky looked up at me from the floor of my bedroom. She was surrounded by cardboard, paint and Textas.

'As many as we can make in a day.' I dumped a box of scissors, glue, glitter and second-hand tinsel next to her on the floor. 'I wanna wallpaper this town with posters advertising the grand opening of our B & B. In fact, I wanna wallpaper Pinebark Ridge, Acacia Falls and Jacaranda Tops as well.'

Becky frowned. 'That's a lot of wallpaper.'

'Don't worry, we'll have an extra pair of hands. Someone will be here to help before you can say "Eggbutt Snaffle".'

'Pree?'

'You bet your bridle!'

Becky punched her fist in the air. 'Yes!'

The doorbell rang. Becky and I scrambled down the stairs in our joddies and socks and flung open the door.

'Pree!' we cried at once, throwing our arms around Priyanka Prasad's neck.

'How cool,' Pree gasped. 'A group hug. I love group hugs. You can never get enough group hugs. Stop me if you've heard this one. Where do you take a sick pony? To the horsepital! D'you get it? To the horsepital!'

Becky and I giggled as we untangled ourselves. Pree's jokes were only slightly better than Gary's, but they always made us smile.

'Come inside,' I said, tugging at Pree's hand. 'We're all ready to start.'

'Where's Jasmine?' Becky said, craning her neck out the front door in search of Pree's fat dun mare.

'Last time I rode all the way out here from the Ridge it took me an hour. I figured if you wanted me here before dinner it might be a better idea to get a lift from Dad. He's so funny. You know he was asleep last night on the lounge and he was snoring and—'

'C'mon,' I said. 'Posters, remember?'

We climbed the stairs.

'Hey, guys, how do you cure a horse with constipation?'

'How?' Becky said, eyebrows raised.

'Put 'em in a horse float. D'you get it? In a horse float! You know how they always go as soon as they set hoof in a horse—'

'We get it,' I said, unable to stop the huge grin that was spreading across my face. Pree is such a good friend. I'll never forget the way she stood up for me at that terrible gymkhana when Becky and I weren't talking. And how she didn't make me join Pinebark Ridge Riding Club even though I said I would. Only a true friend would do something like that.

A few hours, a jumbo bag of nacho cheese corn chips, three cans of cola and three double helpings of fruit salad and ice cream later, no less than twenty posters advertising the grand opening of Miller Lodge (a week away and counting!) were spread across my bedroom floor. My friends and I admired our handiwork.

'This'll get you heaps of customers,' Pree said. 'You'll be beating 'em off with a stick.'

'That may not be good for business,' I laughed. 'But I know what you mean.'

'I'll put one up at the restaurant,' Becky said, scratching at a splodge of orange paint on her nose.

'I'll get Dad to put one up at his surgery,' Pree said, her smile so big her teeth lit up the room. Pree has the whitest teeth I've ever seen. 'And I know! I'll tell Mum to put one up at the stud. We get heaps of people from out of town coming to buy horses and they all need somewhere to stay overnight. Mum's even let 'em crash with us if the hotel's booked out.'

Becky's eyes looked dreamy. 'I can't believe you have a stud. An Arabian stud.'

Pree shrugged. 'It's not as glamorous as it sounds. All I ever get to do is muck out stables, and Arab poo looks just the same as any other horse's poo. Trust me.'

'Well,' I said. 'I don't know about you two, but I need a fix.'

'What do you need to fix?' Pree said, scrunching up her eyebrows.

'I need *a* fix,' I said. 'A horse fix. Who's with me?'

I held out my hand. Becky grabbed it. Pree grabbed Becky's and we shook.

★ ★ ★

'I'll never get it.' I glared at the four empty milk crates we had set up in the paddock in a long L-shape (three in a long straight row then a fourth at a right angle) as markers. All I had to do was walk halfway, from the first crate to the second, then get Honey to jog to the third crate, turn left and keep jogging to the fourth, where I'd stop for judging. That's when it got tricky. I buried my face in Honey's neck and groaned. 'I just can't understand the quarter method. And if no one gets this mini out from under my feet, I'll break my neck as well!'

'What d'you care about the whatever method, anyway?' Pree said.

I sighed. 'I wanna do the Breed Class at the Western Show. You have to know the quarter method to enter.'

'It's a way of moving around the horse while the judge is, well, judging,' Becky said. 'Keeps the judge safe.'

'Gary mentioned it at—'

'Toffee!' Pree shrieked. She was sitting under Honey's tree, Gary's old Western book open on her lap. 'Here, boy!'

'He's not a dog, Pree,' Becky said, re-wrapping her scarf around her neck.

'You wanna bet?' Pree giggled as Toffee bounced away from under Honey's belly and almost dived into her lap. He rolled onto his back and grunted. 'D'you reckon his leg would kick if I scratched his tummy?'

'The quarter method!' I moaned. 'Can we get back on track?'

'It sounds so easy.' Becky collapsed under Honey's tree with Pree and sighed. 'You have to imagine the horse is cut into four. Just like it says in this book.'

'But where's the line? How big are the pieces?' I shook my head and tapped my right temple, trying to wake up my brain.

'This is all so new.' Pree threw a stick for Toffee. He scrambled to his feet and barrelled away across the paddock after it. Pree flicked through the pages of Gary's book. 'You know, I tried to get Jazz to jog the other day and I just couldn't sit down in the saddle. I *had* to do a rising trot. It was like my body was possessed by the ghost of English riding past or something.'

'Tell me about it,' Becky grumbled. 'I can't get my legs to behave either. I don't reckon I'll be ready on time.'

'I don't think I'll do the Western riding classes at all,' I said, rubbing Honey's nose. 'We'll just do a led class. But I'm entering Beginner/Youth Showmanship whether I like it or not. It's the easiest level. I hope that counts for something. And I won't have to ride.' I sighed. 'At least there's barrel racing.'

'Try the Breed Class thing again,' Becky said. 'This time I'll be the judge. Pree, you tell us if we're doing it right.'

'Why me?' Pree wailed, taking the stick from Toffee's mouth and hurling it away again. 'I'm just as English as you are!'

'Think Western!' Becky jogged over to the judge's position at the fourth marker.

'Go to the starting position,' Pree called. I stood beside Honey, holding her lead rope under her chin with my right hand and gathered up the end of the rope with my left. I led her to the first crate.

'Okay, now what?' I said.

'Walk her to the second marker then jog to and around the third marker and to the judge at the fourth.'

'C'mon, Honey,' I said softly, taking a step forward. Honey followed, like a lamb. We walked to the second marker and I prepared for the jog. Well, I hoped Honey would jog. I knew I could, but would she? After all, we'd only had one real Western lesson.

'Get up, Honey,' I murmured, tugging gently on the lead rope. I bounced into a slow jog and Honey followed suit. I kept her moving past and around the third marker and all the way to Becky who gave me the thumbs up.

'What now?' I called.

'Um,' Pree said, leafing through pages of the book. 'Sorry, I was looking at the pictures and I lost, oh, here it is. Do a 360 degree turn then set the horse up for inspection.'

'Turn right or left?' I said.

'Um, right!'

I had allowed Honey to stop too close to Becky. If I turned her in a 360, she'd wipe out my best friend with her rump. I pulled the lead rope straight back towards Honey's chest and clucked my tongue.

'That's a girl!' I said as Honey took three steps backwards.

I took a step to the right, almost directly in front of her nose and pulled gently on the lead rope. She followed me around, doing a 360 degree turn with such precision she should have been wearing a tutu.

We stopped in front of Becky again. I tugged and pushed on the lead rope, hoping to mould Honey into the perfect, straight, square position. She was mostly straight, so I stood beside her, smiled at the judge (aka my best mate — it's good to be best mates with the judge) and waited to be inspected. This was the part I dreaded most — the quarter method.

As Becky stepped to the right and looked at Honey, I stayed on the left. Suddenly, there was a *whooshing* sound just above my head and in less than a second Toffee had belted right through my legs. Everything slowed down for a moment, just like in a movie. I fell backwards, throwing Honey's lead rope up into the air. I made a grab at Becky and pulled her over. She struggled, we twisted in midair and finally landed in the grass in a tangle of arms, legs and lead rope.

'Sorry!' Pree called. 'He wanted me to chuck the stick.'

'He's not a dog!' Becky groaned. 'I can't breathe, Ash!'

'How'd we do?' I said, wrenching my arm out from under Becky's neck and unfolding the rest of me.

'I'm pretty sure that'll win you last place, Ash!' Pree called, giggling.

'So am I!' shrieked a horrible voice from over the fence.

'Why don't you just get lost, Ratbag?' I helped Becky to her feet and dusted her off. This was no way to impress a judge. I was a Western rookie, but I knew that first-place ribbons weren't won by knocking a judge unconscious.

'I could, but it's more fun watching youse two making total dopes of yourselves.'

'Ignore him,' I boomed, brushing down my joddies with my hands. 'C'mon, Honey. Let's try again.'

I led her back to the starting point and began the pattern again. The walk, the jog, the 360 — everything was perfect, right up until the quarter method. This time I tripped over my own feet and ended up nose to toes with Becky. I couldn't even blame Toffee. He was chasing his tail by the fence, snapping at it with his teeth.

Flea clapped and whistled. 'What a champion! You'll win Boofhead Under Saddle this year for sure!'

'Think you can do better?' I shrieked, picking grass from my mouth.

'Matter of fact, I do.'

With that, Flea jumped the fence and sauntered across the yard.

'What're you doing on my lawn?' I yelled.

Flea wasn't bothered. He jumped the paddock fence and in less than a heartbeat had his grotty hands on my Honey's lead rope. I glowered at him, clinging to the lead. I wasn't going to give my Honey up. No way. And I really wasn't all that happy being in our paddock with one of my sworn enemies. I had made it one of my personal goals to stay as far away from Flea as I could. Considering we shared a fence, a Riding Club, a Year Six class and a small country town — that was almost impossible.

'Let go,' I snarled through clenched teeth, surprised that any noise had escaped from them at all.

Flea grinned. I winced. So much sludge coated his teeth he could have been arrested for crimes against dentistry.

'I wanna help youse.'

I gave Flea my most menacing glare. 'No you don't.'

'I do. I've done this before.' Flea looked into my eyes and for the first time I saw that there was more to him than messy hair and filthy joddies. Call me crazy, but I let go of the lead rope.

He grinned and winked. 'It's like this. In

Showmanship the judge wants to see the horse from every angle. Okay?'

I nodded, still looking at him a little suspiciously. What had come over him? He'd hated me from my first day in Shady Creek. Why was he suddenly Mr Helpful?

'Cut the horse down the middle and then in half in your head, so that you have four quarters. Have you done that?'

I nodded again.

'As the judge moves around the horse you move to the safe quarter. Stand by the part of the horse opposite to the judge.' Flea beamed, triumphant.

'Why?' I hadn't noticed, but Pree had joined us and was all ears.

Flea cleared his throat. 'If the horse mucks up you move the horse away from the judge and take them out of danger. It's that simple. Watch.'

Flea ordered Pree to be the judge. He held Honey by the lead rope, and stood on her left, or nearside.

'I'm on the nearside, so you're on the offside,' he said.

Pree stood on Honey's off, or right, side.

'Now come to her nearside.'

Pree took a few steps left and Flea moved right gracefully.

'Again,' he said.

They swapped sides over and over until I really thought I understood.

'Now I'll be the judge.' Flea offered me Honey's lead rope. I took it and stared first at the rope and then at him. This was all too weird. He was either very sick or was under the influence of hypnosis. It could even have been hormones. Whatever it was, I hoped it never, ever wore off.

Flea, as the judge, moved to each of Honey's quarters and each time I stepped into her safe quarter, ready, just in case she misbehaved.

Becky nodded, smiling. 'I think you've got it, Ash. Thank goodness!'

'Good job,' Pree said. 'And you two make a great team. You should think about—'

'No!' Flea and I burst out at once. Whatever it was she'd been about to suggest it could never happen. Not in this lifetime. Not with Flea!

'That's all folks,' Flea said, ambling away.

'Hey!' I called after him.

He looked at me over his shoulder, squinting into the afternoon sun.

'Thanks.' I unbuckled Honey's halter and let it slip over her nose.

'No worries,' he said. 'Good luck at the show, Spiller!'

'I knew it was too good to be true,' I said as he jumped the fence again and disappeared.

Becky slung her arm around my shoulder. 'I believe we've all been witnesses to a miracle.'

I fell to my knees and looked up at the sky. 'Thank you, horse gods!'

'I wonder if they really exist?' Pree murmured. 'You know, these horse gods of yours.'

'We've only gotta look at our horses to know that something out there loves us,' Becky mused.

A car horn beeped. Doctor Prasad had pulled into the driveway. Pree gave Becky and me a quick hug.

'I've got one for you!' she called as she waved goodbye. 'Why did the rodeo horse get so rich? He had a lot of bucks. D'you get it? Bucks!'

Becky and I watched Pree and her dad drive away.

'I have to go, too,' Becky said. 'It's almost time to open Rebecca's Garden up for dinner and I have to be there.'

'You know, if you ever need a waitress or someone to help out, just call me,' I said, as Becky bounced onto Charlie's back. 'Horse Cents can always use the cash flow.'

'You're on!' Becky grinned and touched her forefinger to her helmet. 'See ya!'

I waved until she and Charlie had disappeared around the corner, then checked on my horses. As Honey grazed, Toffee nipped at her tail then ran for his life. Honey looked at him, shook her head and went back to her snack, just like a patient mum.

I blew them a kiss each and jogged up the back stairs and into the kitchen then down the hallway and into Dad's office. It had been a few days since I'd checked my emails and I was hoping to hear from Jenna. I missed her *so* much and days like these, with Beck and Pree, only made things worse. I wanted her here with me, sharing our fun. Not miles and miles away from home. The months she had been away in Italy had seemed more like years, decades even.

I flopped into Dad's chair and turned on the computer. It hummed instantly and a green light winked and blinked at me. I drummed my fingers, waiting for the desktop to appear, then I clicked on *Mail*. There was a message from Jenna!

'At last,' I murmured. 'What's she been up to?'

I drank in the words, then pushed the chair away from the desk and ran from the room. I wanted to scream, shout, jump, dance. I wanted to do it all! But Dad and his paint tins got in my way.

'What's going on?' Dad grumbled, picking up his jumbo tin of Peach Satin Finish.

'It's the best!' I cried. 'The best news since, I dunno. Since Jenna came to stay for the summer holidays.'

'What is it?' Dad's eyes were wide. 'What could be better than that?'

'Jenna wants to come for the next school holidays. She wants to stay here with us. She can be here for my birthday! Can she stay with us, Dad? Oh, please, please, please?'

'We'll see,' he said. I knew him well enough to know that *we'll see* means yes. Definitely yes.

I hugged him tight around his neck and ran back outside. I had to tell Honey.

eight

Miller Lodge

'Your posters have done the trick, girls. This party's getting down!'

'Dad!' I groaned. 'No one says "getting down" any more.'

Dad looked shocked. 'They don't? Are you sure?'

Pree nodded solemnly. 'Sorry, Mr Miller. People just don't get down these days.'

'Are you saying I'm out of touch? I thought I was so hip!'

I slapped my hands against my face. 'Dad! No one says "hip" any more!'

Dad slumped into a green plastic lawn chair and pretended to sob. I patted his back.

'Bad luck, Mr M,' Becky said, shaking her head. 'But it happens to all of you eventually.'

Dad's sobs dried up at once. 'What happens? To all of who?'

'You parents,' I said, poking his arm. 'You all get old and start embarrassing your poor children.'

Dad sighed and slapped his hands on his legs. 'Well, before I get any older and embarrass you girls even more than I already have, I'd better see to the barbie.'

He disappeared into the crowds of people who had come from all over the district to celebrate the grand opening of Miller Lodge. Becky, Pree and I had wallpapered the town with our posters and, apart from the few we'd found with *Miller Lodge* changed to *Spiller Splodge* (no prizes for guessing who was behind that!), they'd been a huge success.

The whole day had been planned to the last detail. Becky, Pree and I were conducting tours of Miller Lodge every half-hour. People 'oohed' at our guest rooms, the dining room and the entertainment room. They 'ahhed' at the pool, the barbecue area and the stable. They 'oohed' and 'ahhed' at Honey and Toffee. They 'coocheecooed' at Jason, who looked even more gorgeous than usual in a Miller Lodge cap.

Pree, Becky and I were munching on our second steak sandwiches (with tomato sauce and extra onions) when I told them my totally awesome news.

'You're kidding!' Becky said. 'When's she coming?'

'Next school holidays.' I couldn't help but smile. 'And we all know what's happening then. Have I mentioned that I'm turning twelve?'

'Nah,' Becky said, rolling her eyes.

'So I'm finally gonna meet Jenna Dawson,' Pree said. '*The* Jenna.'

'Yup,' I said. 'D'you reckon she can ride Cassata again while she's here?'

Becky shrugged. 'Dunno. Now that Rachael is finally normal she wants her all the time. She won't even let me ride her now. She keeps going on about how when I ride Cassata I *un-teach* her.' Becky pulled a face. 'Rachael seems to have a pretty bad case of amnesia. For two years, up until Cassata was stolen, I did everything for her.'

'Well, maybe Jenna could—'

'I don't believe it!' Becky said suddenly.

'What?' Had Flea tipped washing detergent into our sparkling blue and frog-free (thanks to me) pool?

Becky hid behind her sandwich. 'Those McMurray girls. Over there.'

'Oh no!' I couldn't believe it. Of all the B & B openings in all the world, they had to walk into mine! 'What do I do?'

'Keep still. They're like lions. Once you run, they'll chase you down.'

Becky and I huddled behind Pree for a few minutes until the McMurrays had stalked past. I could hear Savannah complaining about the food, the weather and the stable. My fingers curled tight around my steak sandwich.

'Hey, what do you call a horse with no ears?' Pree said at last.

I shrugged. 'What?'

'Anything!' Pree doubled over, laughing. Becky and I joined in. We sat together swapping jokes and laughing and having a great time until Mum came over and poked me in the ribs.

'People have been asking about pony rides.'

I swallowed so hard my eyes watered. 'What about them?'

Mum's face was intent. 'People want pony rides for their kids. Be a good girl and saddle up Honey for me, will you?'

I took a small bite and glanced at Becky. She raised her eyebrows. 'I don't think that's such a hot idea.'

Mum frowned. 'Why not? Some of these people will be making bookings depending on how much they enjoy today. We need bookings, and may I remind you that you are part of the "we".'

I wiped at my mouth with the back of my hand. 'But, Mum.'

Mum folded her arms. Her ears went red, just the way they always do when she gets mad. I could tell this was going to end badly.

'I don't want to use Honey for pony rides.' I chewed on my lip.

'Why not?' Mum hissed. 'There are heaps of families here with little kids. The kids want pony rides and you have a pony.'

'She's not a pony. She's 14.2 hands high. That makes her a horse.' I knew I was being cheeky. But I didn't know what to do. I didn't know what to say to make her understand that Honey was all mine. I could share Honey with Jason or Pree or Becky or Jenna. But I loved them. I thought about all those strangers bouncing on her back and pulling at her mouth and shuddered.

Mum smiled tightly at Pree and Becky. 'Would you excuse us for a moment, please, girls?'

They gave me a sympathetic look and wandered

over to the face-painting table that Rachael Cho had been running as a special opening present to us.

'How could you be so rude to me in front of your friends?' Mum said. Her face was red. Her ears were almost luminous.

'Honey's *my* horse,' I said. 'I'm the one who found her. I'm the one who saved her. I'm the one who works my butt off to pay for her and you never help me.'

Mum's eyes widened. Her ears were flashing now, like Christmas lights. I stared at my steak sandwich, wishing I could take back everything I'd just said. Not because I didn't mean it. After all, of all the kids in Shady Creek with horses of their own, I was the only one who had to worry about how to pay farriers and pray that I'd never have to call Amanda Filano, the local vet. I was the only one who knew which produce stores sold the cheapest lucerne hay and where to get the best quality second-hand tack. Mum and Dad had promised to help me out before. But then Mum had Jason and now Dad had left his job.

I love looking after Honey and Toffee and I am proud that, so far, I've managed to do it all with Horse Cents. But sometimes I wish that I was just like Lauren Landon — the rich girl whose dad had bought Cassata for her at that terrible auction — and that I never have to worry about money again.

'I just don't understand what's happening to you, Ash.' Mum shook her head and took a step backwards. 'Sometimes it's like I don't know you any more.'

'I'll tack Jazz up for you, Mrs Miller,' Pree said, reappearing suddenly with a huge pink flower painted on each of her cheeks. 'She could do with the exercise.'

Mum gave her a small smile. 'Thank you, Pree.'

Mum's eyes fell on mine and I could see how much I'd let her down. I knew I needed to apologize. Problem was, I didn't know how. I knew how to open my mouth and speak of course, and I definitely knew what the word *sorry* meant and how to say it. But something big had happened between Mum and me. It was like I'd climbed so far up a mountain that it was easier to keep going up than to turn around and go back down.

Miller Lodge was quiet. The grand opening was over and all that was left to do was clean up the mess and wait for the phone to ring.

I'd decided that the best way I could make up with Mum was to do chores. So far I'd vacuumed the whole bottom floor, taken out the garbage and started washing up the dinner dishes (for free!).

Mum had hardly said anything to me all afternoon. At least when I was vacuuming she'd had a good reason not to talk to me. But now it was just the two of us in the kitchen and neither of us had said a word. I felt all wriggly and yucky. I was relieved when she went upstairs to give Jason his bedtime bottle.

Dad wandered in and collapsed onto a chair just as I stacked the last plate on the dish rack.

'How goes it, Ash?'

'Hmm.' I wiped the bench with a tea towel and hung it over the oven door handle to dry.

'What's "Hmm"?' he said, reaching into the fruit bowl for an orange. 'These are so good, straight from the tree. Mind you, I'm surprised Mrs Adams keeps bringing them over after what Toffee did to her corn.'

'We're doing her a favour taking them off her hands. She lives alone. Can you imagine what'd happen if she kept all those oranges for herself?' I giggled, imagining Mrs Adams bouncing across a sea of oranges like a sheepdog bouncing across a sea of woolly sheep.

'We should add them to the breakfast menu.' Dad's eyes glazed over. 'Organic freshly squeezed orange juice. Perfect with bacon and free-range eggs.'

I cleared my throat. 'Speaking of the B & B, I've got an idea. You know, about our potential clientele.'

Dad raised his eyebrows and for a second I thought he was smiling. 'Planning for the future of the business. Just what I like to see from one of the company directors.'

'Well, I thought that seeing as how there are so many horse shows around here and how people from all over the district come and compete, maybe you could advertise on the show programmes. You could say that we have stabling, a corral and paddocks. That way they could—'

'Stay overnight!' Dad beamed. 'Much better for the horses to be rested before the long drive home. Ash, you're a genius!'

'But you know, Dad, it's better for guest horses to be separate from Honey and Toff. They could fight or get sick.'

Dad ripped the orange in half and took a huge

bite. I wrinkled my nose, shaking my head when he offered me a share.

'You'll never guess!' Mum ran into the kitchen clutching the brand new Miller Lodge register. She was all lit up. 'We got a booking! Our first booking. They want both guest rooms. They're coming this weekend.'

'Lemme see.' Dad grabbed the register from her hands and pointed to the entry. 'I told you. Didn't I tell you? We'll make this work, Helen. I know we will.'

'There's just one thing,' Mum said. Her expression changed. 'They're bringing a horse. I said no problem. I mean, we can accommodate another horse, right? It's only for one night.'

Dad patted my back, grinning. 'Ash already has that one figured out. Right?'

I nodded, still torn between being mad at Mum over the pony rides idea and feeling ashamed of the way I'd reacted.

Mum wrapped her arms around me and held me close for a long moment. I stopped resisting and just allowed myself to be rocked.

'That's my girl,' Mum murmured. 'My gorgeous girl.'

I wanted to tell her how sorry I was and how much I loved her. But my throat was tight and I was having trouble swallowing. Instead I cried. Not great racking sobs, but warm, gentle tears that, like a valve, released the pressure just enough to make me feel better. I wrapped my arms around Mum and hugged her back.

nine

Employee of the Week

'Ash, love, I need you to try harder with the girls.'
Mrs McMurray watched me intently from her chair.
I usually loved being in her office. The smell of the
new carpet still lingered. Soft sweet classical music
whispered from the stereo unit. Pictures of horses
covered the walls. It was an easy, friendly place to be.
Usually.

'I did try,' I said in a small voice. I stared at my
hands, avoiding her eyes. Maybe it was me. Maybe I
hadn't given them a chance. Maybe they'd been
jetlagged. Maybe it was because they were new. I
remembered only too well what it was like to be
new. I'd let Mrs Mac down and that was something
I'd never wanted to do. After all, if it hadn't been for

her we'd never have got Cassata back. I'd never be able to keep Horse Cents running. And I wouldn't have such an awesome place to ride and work. I owed her a lot. I owed her being nice to her granddaughters, anyway.

'It took days for me to convince them that the Shady Boa was a figment of your rather mischievous imagination.' Mrs McMurray sighed and touched her lips with her fingertips. I'd come to know that she always did this when she was thinking. 'And at the grand opening of Miller Lodge, I had the feeling you were trying to avoid them.'

'It's just—'

'I told them all about you and they were really looking forward to meeting you, Ash.'

Before I could stop myself I was chewing on my fingernails. I wished that Jenna was here already. She'd be on my side. She'd know what to do. 'But I was busy that day, I was . . .' I couldn't say I was doing pony rides. 'I was helping Mum and Dad.'

Mrs Mac watched me for a moment. I prayed with all my heart to the horse gods. *Please don't let her be a mind-reader.* 'What's Sam got in store for you today?'

'Tack. I'm cleaning tack with Pree.'

'I reckon the girls'd love to help you two out. Whaddya say?'

Mrs Mac turned her music up, which I knew was her way of saying that our meeting was over. I hadn't taken two steps from her office when someone tapped my shoulder.

'Did you get into trouble? Did you?'

I folded my arms and glowered at Savannah McMurray. 'Of course not.'

'Ha!' she cried, clapping her hands. 'I knew you would. I knew Nanna would be cross. I knew I'd make her get mad at you.'

'Where's your sister?' I said, sourly. 'Germproofing your room?'

Savannah grew serious. 'You'd better watch what you say. All I need to do is tell Nanna and you'll be kicked out of Shady Trails faster than the top land speed of a Shady Boa.'

I turned my back on her and headed for the stables. 'They can be pretty fast.'

Savannah skipped after me. 'Nanna said I can hang around with you *all* day.'

I rolled my eyes. 'I can't wait.'

We reached the stables and I turned left, making a beeline for the tack room. It was tack-cleaning day.

Every saddle, every bridle — every piece of gear — had to be thoroughly checked and cleaned. Some people hate cleaning tack. But I love it. Especially when I get to do it with Pree — on those days I go home with my cheeks aching from laughing so hard.

I scuttled past the long row of horses, some with their noses firmly camped in their feed bins, others with their sweet heads sticking out over their stall gates so they could have a good stickybeak at the goings-on at Shady Trails.

I opened the tack room door. The Trails tack room is amazing. One of the walls is lined with saddles of all styles and designs. Each saddle sits on its own neat black metal saddle rack. The horse's or pony's name is engraved on a black metal plate and fixed to the wall above the saddle rack. Saddlecloths are tucked under the saddles. The bridles hang in long tidy rows from round, black metal bridle racks mounted on the opposite wall. I love visiting the tack room. It's so horsy and smells so delicious.

'Hey!' Pree was sitting on a stool with a saddle balanced on her lap, rubbing saddle soap into the seat with a damp sponge. Her face lit up. 'Ash! I've got one for you. What do you give a horse with a

cold? Cough stirrup! D'you get it? Cough stirrup!'
Pree dissolved into giggles.

I couldn't help but smile. There's something about
Pree that makes me warm inside.

'That was the worst joke I've ever heard.'
Savannah pushed past me and into the tack room.
Pree's face darkened.

'Savannah, this is Pree Prasad,' I said.

Pree stood up, the saddle wedged between her
knees and her chest, and held out her non-sponged
hand. Her thick black plait was so long it touched
the waistband of her dark blue joddies. 'So you're—'

'Savannah McMurray.' She folded her arms and
glowered at Pree. 'As in Mrs McMurray's
granddaughter.'

Pree sat down again and smiled, the kind of smile
I knew meant she understood. 'I thought so. Here ...'
Pree threw her sponge at Savannah. 'Make yourself
useful.'

Savannah let the sponge fall at her feet and stared
at Pree with her mouth open. 'And what exactly do
you want me to do?'

'Clean Calypso's saddle,' Pree said. She pointed to
a black leather all-purpose saddle sitting neatly on a
saddle rack. 'And once you do that one you can get

started on the rest.' Pree made a sweeping movement with her hand, a bit like a game-show host gesturing at a stack of glittering prizes.

'I'm not a worker,' Savannah cried. 'This isn't what I'm here for!'

'Tell you what,' I said, 'why don't we make it a race?'

Savannah's expression changed in an instant. 'A race?'

I nodded, trying to appear as enthusiastic as I could. 'A race. The person with the most saddles cleaned by the end of the morning is the Employee of the Week.'

'Employee of the Week?' Savannah licked her lips.

I nodded again. 'Uh huh.'

'Will I get a prize?' Savannah's eyes were hungry.

I snorted. 'Only if you win. You've got some pretty hot competition here.'

Savannah clapped her hands. 'I'll win. I'll win for sure. I *always* win. I'm one of those people who wins *everything*!'

'Ever cleaned a saddle?' Pree said, giving me a knowing look.

Savannah shook her head. 'Of course not. That's what stablehands are for. I'm a rider, not a cleaner.'

Pree's mouth dropped open. I stepped in.

'It's easy.' I took a saddle from the wall. The plate above it said *Bartok*. I sat on an empty stool and placed the saddle over my lap.

'All leather saddles need a coat of leather dressing once a month, but we did that two weeks ago. Today we're only cleaning.'

'Okay, okay,' said Savannah, hopping from foot to foot.

Pree pointed out the door. 'The toilet's that way.'

Savannah rolled her eyes and let out her breath. 'I want to get started. I want to win this.'

'Then you'd better listen,' I said. 'What would happen if you cleaned the most saddles but did them all wrong and had to start again? Pree or I could finish first after all.'

Savannah's face changed colour, like being beaten by either Pree or me was the worst thing that could possibly happen to her. I knew I had her complete attention.

'First, wipe the saddle down with a damp cloth.' I dipped a rag kept just for cleaning tack into the bucket of warm water Pree had been using, squeezed out the excess and wiped the entire saddle. 'This gets rid of any grease or dirt.'

Savannah eyed the pile of rags. She was almost salivating.

'Then, take the saddle soap,' I said, leaning down and picking up Pree's bar and sponge. 'And soap up a damp sponge.'

I rubbed it against Pree's sponge until it was nice and soapy.

'Now what?' Savannah looked from her watch to the wall of saddles.

'Give the saddle a good clean with the sponge, inside and out. Don't use too much soap or the saddle acts like a dirt-catcher and you wind up with stained joddies.' I rubbed the sponge on the saddle seat. 'Make sure you do the sweat flap and girth straps as well. Then rub the whole thing down with a clean dry cloth.'

'Is that all? Ha! That's so easy!'

'That's all until we clean the bridles,' said Pree, replacing the saddle she'd cleaned and collecting another. 'By the way. I'm one up on you now.'

That was all it took. Savannah went into a saddle-cleaning frenzy. By mid-morning she'd cleaned nine saddles.

'You can stop now,' I said. 'It's time for our morning tea break.'

Savannah shook her head and brushed mud from Hector's girth. 'No.'

I took the girth in my hand. 'Have a break.'

Savannah snatched the girth away from me so hard, my skin stung. 'How many saddles have you done?'

'Four,' I said.

'Five.' Pree nudged me with her elbow.

Savannah frowned and laid the girth strap over Hector's saddle, then removed his stirrup leathers and wiped them with her cloth. 'Then I have no choice. I have to keep going. You two are the only things standing between me and being Employee of the Week.'

Suddenly I felt all squirmy inside, like something slimy was wriggling around inside my guts.

'You've done almost twice as many as either of us.' I tapped her shoulder. She was sweaty and hot. 'Come and have a drink.'

'You must be kidding!' Savannah bared her teeth. 'You're just waiting for me to stop so you can try to catch up. Do I look like I was born yesterday?'

'There's no Employee of the Week,' I admitted. 'I made it up.'

Savannah dropped the stirrup irons into a bucket of warm, soapy water. 'You're just saying that because you don't want me to win!'

'It's true. That part, anyway. I was just—'

'Could you bring me something to eat? Nanna wouldn't be happy if I didn't have morning tea.' Savannah rubbed soap into the stirrup leather.

Pree and I exchanged glances. She'd been working so hard, it was only right that we brought something back for her. The last thing I wanted after my chat with Mrs Mac was for Savannah to collapse from tack-cleaning exhaustion.

'No problem,' I said. I tugged at Pree's elbow. 'We'll be back soon.'

Savannah gave us a quick smile. 'I'll be here.'

We headed for the staff room where we knew drinks, biscuits and fruit were waiting for us. Mrs McMurray really looked after us. We brought our own lunches, but morning and afternoon tea was always her treat.

Pree and I stuffed ourselves with cream-filled biscuits and Pree entertained everyone with her latest joke about how if everyone had a horse the country would be more stable.

'Back to the tack room,' Sam said at the end of our break, shooing us out of the staff room with her fingers. I snatched three bananas from the fruit bowl while Pree scooped up three juice boxes.

Provisions in hand, we jogged back to the tack room to find it locked from the inside.

'Are you in there?' I called, banging on the door. 'Open up, we brought you morning tea!'

'A likely story,' Savannah cried. I could hear her scrubbing something.

'Open the door,' Pree yelled. 'You're the winner. You're the Employee of the Week.'

'I don't believe you.' Savannah's scrubbing became more frantic. 'You're trying to trick me.'

I swallowed hard and dumped the bananas on top of a feed bin. 'This has gone too far. I have to get Mrs McMurray.'

Pree nodded. 'You run up to the office, I'll try to talk her out.'

If anyone could talk someone out, it was Pree.

I turned and ran and within a few minutes Mrs McMurray was standing outside the door with us.

'What happened?' she said, panting.

I told her everything. She looked into my eyes. I'd never seen her look so disappointed.

'Ashleigh, I'm amazed you could do such a thing.' Her face was red and her lips were thin.

My face burned.

'Mrs McMurray, it wasn't only Ash. I did it as well.' Pree's eyes were solemn. 'Please don't be mad. We were only playing around. We didn't know this would happen.'

'Savvy, darl,' Mrs McMurray called. 'Unlock the door. Ashleigh and Priyanka have something to say to you.'

The lock clicked and the door opened a crack. Savannah peeped out. 'Did I win? Am I Employee of the Week?'

'You won,' I said softly. Savannah had been a pain, but I felt terrible.

'I won?' Savannah threw the door open. Her hair was damp and her cheeks were flushed. The floor of the tack room was strewn with bridles. 'Ha! I'm Employee of the Week! Ha!' She clapped her hands. 'I knew I'd win. I'm a winner. I'm the best at everything!'

Mrs McMurray cleared her throat. 'Ash? Pree?' She gave us a look. A look that said we weren't out of danger yet.

'Sorry,' I said.

'Me too.' Pree scuffed her riding boot against the stable floor.

'I told you I'm the best and you know why?' Savannah clapped her hands again. 'I cleaned all the saddles and then I did the bridles.'

'But we didn't show you how to do the bridles,' I said. 'How'd you clean them?'

'I took off all the bits and polished them with this bottle of stuff I found here, but I still have to put them all back on the bridles.' Savannah beamed, pleased with herself.

My heart plunged. 'Bottle of what stuff?'

Savannah picked her way through the bridles and returned with a bottle of metal polish.

'You didn't use this, did you?' Pree wailed. 'You should never use metal polish on bits!'

Mrs McMurray smiled at us. 'I reckon you two girls have some cleaning to do.' She slipped her arm around Savannah's shoulders and, saying something about a nice hot drink, steered her back towards the office.

Pree and I surveyed the damage.

'How many bits d'you reckon we have here?' I said, staring at the floor. It was like a bridle factory.

'Hundreds,' said Pree. 'Thousands, maybe.'

Pree caught my look and held up her hands. 'Okay, okay. Maybe there's a few dozen or so.'

I rolled my eyes. 'How're we s'posed to know which bit goes with which bridle?'

'Dunno.' Pree shrugged. 'But we deserve it. Hey, I've got one for you. What's a horse's favourite game? Stable tennis. D'you get it? Stable tennis!'

I giggled, plucking my first bridle from the floor. I sat on my stool and began sorting through the bits while Pree hurried to refill the bucket with clean warm water.

ten

Return of the King

'Are you sure?' I snatched the guest register from Mum and read the name again and again. 'Are you really sure?'

'Knock it off, Ash! They'll be here any minute. They're our first guests and I want everything to be perfect.'

'Mum!' I wailed. 'Don't you understand? If they're who I think they are nothing will be good enough. Even if we served them breakfast on crystal plates they wouldn't be happy.'

Dad snapped his fingers. 'Now you're talking! Helen, where are those dreadful crystal goblets we got from your Aunt Ethel as a wedding present?'

Mum wrinkled her nose. 'What in blazes do you want those for?'

Dad sighed. 'For our more, you know, luxury-loving guests. Imagine if we served their water in crystal goblets — fancy schmancy!'

Mum shrugged. 'We used one as a pen holder. And the rest—'

'I sold off in that garage sale. Remember?'

Dad gave me a look. 'Ashleigh, I've tried so hard to put it all behind me. My doctor keeps telling me I have to move on with my life, but how will I ever manage it if you keep bringing up that garage sale?'

'I'm trying to move on with my life as well,' I said, thumping my chest for extra effect. 'I can't spend a night under the same roof as Nicki King. I just can't!'

'It may be another family,' Mum said gently. 'I know you didn't get on with Nicki, but King's a common name.'

'Didn't get on?' I cried. 'Didn't get on? We hated each other. She practically ruined South Beach Stables for me. Leaving Nicki King behind in the city was one of the best things about moving to Shady Creek.'

'Apart from getting Honey,' Mum said.

'And Toffee.' Trust Dad.

'And meeting Becky.' Mum wriggled her nose.

'And joining Shady Creek Riding Club.' Dad whacked my back affectionately.

I held up my hands. 'Okay, okay. It's obvious I'm wasting my time here. But just remember. You were warned!'

A car horn blasted and the three of us jumped in fright.

'Who could that be?' Mum frowned. She'd come to love her peace and quiet so much that she didn't take kindly to it being disturbed. There was another reason she liked things quiet. 'Jason's sleeping.'

The horn blasted again and Dad rushed to the front door. He opened it, stuck his head out and waved at us frantically.

I could hear car doors slamming and voices. Dad opened the door wide and a tall man with very dark hair in a blue business suit strode into the hall. He was followed by a small woman with dark glasses and a girl, about my age, whose strawberry blonde hair was cropped to her shoulders. She fluffed it out with her fingers and smiled.

'Ashleigh Miller! Fancy seeing you running a moth-eaten hotel.'

'Nicki,' I smiled through clenched teeth, impressed with myself for managing to say her name at all.

The tall man snapped his fingers. 'Porter, bring our luggage in at once.'

Dad arched one copper-coloured eyebrow and shrugged, then set off outside. Mum coughed and opened the guest register.

'King family.' Mum said, a tight smile pulling at her face. 'So nice to see you again. For one night?'

'That's right,' Mr King said. He put his arm around Nicki's shoulders. 'Have your stablehand attend to my daughter's horse. He's a very valuable animal. I hope your stabling facilities are in order.'

Mum nodded. 'Perfectly in order.' She gave me a look. 'Ash, see to Nicki's horse, please.'

I sighed. I just couldn't believe it. Nicki King right here in my house. I racked my brains frantically, trying to remember which really terrible thing I'd done in this life that I was now being tormented for. Maybe I was being tormented in advance for something I hadn't done yet. 'Yes, Mum.'

Nicki smirked at me from underneath her father's arm. 'I'll go with her, Daddy. It's so good to see Ashleigh again. I don't want to waste a single moment.'

I rolled my eyes and pushed past Dad who was dragging the last of the Kings' matching luggage into the hall. Nicki followed hard on my heels.

'I had the feeling it might be you,' Nicki hissed. 'But I thought you'd moved to Hicksville. Oh, wait a minute!' Nicki's face was alight, as though she'd just had an epiphany. 'This *is* Hicksville!'

'Go roll in a cow pat,' I grumbled under my breath, unbolting the ramp of Nicki's float. It was new and impressive. More like a stable on wheels than a float. But I wasn't going to let Nicki know I liked it. Not for all the pony pellets in Pinebark Ridge!

I peeked inside the float. An immaculate black gelding was waiting. He turned his head towards me, his ears pricked forward and I sucked in my breath. I had never seen such a perfect face.

I lowered the ramp and swung out the bar then ducked under the front bar and unhooked the horse's lead rope from the wall of the float. He was well-dressed for his trip, covered in a sleek, very expensive-looking rug, had matching travel boots and sported a bandaged tail. I pushed gently on his chest and clucked with my tongue.

'Easy!' Nicki cried. 'Prince is worth more than you and your crummy hotel put together.'

'You haven't changed,' I said, easing the horse slowly down the ramp until he was standing in the driveway.

Nicki glared at me and snatched his lead rope. 'That was a mess! I've never seen Prince backed out of the float so sloppily before.'

'I've got an idea for you, Nicki,' I snapped. 'Next time try doing it yourself. Wait a minute — did you just say his name is Prince?'

'Yes,' Nicki said, fluffing out her hair again.

I smiled. 'So your horse's name is Prince King?'

'Correction,' Nicki said, a satisfied smile on her face. 'His name is Paydaprincely Sum King. He's a registered Morgan. The only Morgan at City Stables.'

That was when it hit me with the force of a fly-away feed bin. 'But you had an Arab. A mare called—'

'Jewel. She was after Sonny. Useless.'

'She was gorgeous. I can't believe you got rid of her. I can't believe you got rid of Sonny, either.' What was wrong with this girl? After everything I'd gone through for Honey. With Honey. And Nicki got not one, but three horses just handed to her on a silver snaffle.

I stabled Prince with Nicki watching my every move, then removed his travel boots and tail bandages. I filled a haynet and made sure he had plenty of fresh water, then patted his neck and wished him luck. I could only imagine he wouldn't be spending long with Nicki King.

'So what are you doing around here, anyway?' I said as Nicki sauntered back to the house.

'Not that it's any of your business, but I'm competing in a show. At Winmollong.'

I scrunched up my forehead. I'd heard of Winmollong but had never been there. It seemed a really long way for Nicki to go just to ride in a show. She could do that anytime without having to drive too far from the city where, I knew from our South Beach days, she lived in a huge house by the water.

Nicki seemed to know what I was thinking. 'I knew you wouldn't have a clue, Ashleigh.' She sighed. 'I'm competing for my school. I finally started at St Mary's Ladies College. We have an equestrian team. If I win a place at Winmollong I'll have my photo in the school online newsletter.'

'Congratulations.' I turned my back on Nicki, seized with fear. What if the kids at Linley Heights were all like her? I wouldn't last a day. The whole Linley thing had been a mistake. A terrible mistake.

I gritted my teeth, thinking of the very expensive private girls boarding school Mrs Mac had been so keen for me to apply to. There was no way Mum and Dad could afford to pay the fees. But Linley Heights School offered one riding scholarship for a girl entering Year Seven. I'd almost drooled as I'd read their brochure (Mrs Mac called it a prospectus) and learned all about their riding facilities. But if going to a school like that meant being surrounded by hundreds of Nickis, I'd be better off going to Shady Creek and Districts High School with Becky and Pree.

I slipped between the rails and into Honey's and Toffee's paddock. It was really quite cold and I wanted to check their rugs. Now that the stable was booked for the night it was even more essential that they were warm. I didn't use the stable all that often. Only in freezing or rainy weather or during a storm. But it had always been nice to know it was there if I needed it. I sent up a prayer to the horse gods that there would be no cyclones, blizzards, torrential rains or electrical storms for the next twelve hours. The last thing I wanted was for my horses to get sick. The last thing I needed was a vet bill.

'Get back here!' Nicki yelled. 'You have to hose my float.'

'You know something, Nicki?' I said, tossing words over my shoulder like salt. 'I don't!'

I shivered, even though I was wearing a coat. Not my best thick coat, but my old scruffy one that Mum doesn't mind my getting chaff, horse dribble and mud on. I saw a rugged rump sticking out from behind a tree and smiled. Honey. The love of my life. I needed some serious horse therapy after my Nicki King experience.

I cuddled and kissed her, checked her rug was securely fitted and that the straps hadn't unclipped, and ran my hands down each of her legs, checking for bumps, swellings, heat or tenderness. She nuzzled the back pocket of my jeans, but I held my hands open to show her they were empty.

'Nothing!' I said. 'Sorry. But I'll get your dinner if you like.'

I could have sworn Honey smiled.

I headed for the stable and fixed Honey's dinner of green and white chaff and sliced a carrot into it for good measure. Toffee had the same, but a smaller serve. I loved being with them every moment, and, I have to confess, it was also wonderful being nowhere near Nicki.

It also gave me time to think. There were so many things to worry about — from the Western Show to the McMurrays to all my new B & B jobs — on top of bursting at the seams that Jenna was coming to visit, that I felt like I was riding a wild brumby.

I hauled the two buckets of feed from the stable to the paddock, tipping them into Honey's and Toffee's feed bins. My horses pounced.

'Anyone'd think you hadn't eaten in a week!' I giggled and picked pieces of dry leaves and twigs from Toffee's mane.

Mum finally called the magic word out of the back door and across the paddock. 'Dinner!'

I gave my horses one last pat and scampered home.

eleven

Eqwhine

*'I'm a guest, you're the host. That means you do what I
say and give me what I want!'*

'She really said that?' Becky's voice was soothing,
but I needed her here with me more than ever. The
last time I'd faced Nicki King, Becky had been by
my side. I didn't know if I could survive the night
without her.

'That's only the start of it,' I wailed. 'Her horse
took a huge bite out of our stable wall and instead of
apologizing or even offering to pay for the damage,
she's threatening to sue me. She reckons the wall
gave him indigestion. Can't you sleep over? Please!'

Becky was silent for a moment on the other end
of the phone. 'I wish. But I can't tonight. Dad's

working late and I've got to get to the bottom of this Western thing. This is about my last chance to figure this out before the show.'

'S'pose,' I grumbled. 'But I need you.' I kicked at the freshly painted wall. 'And I don't know why you just don't come out and ask him.'

'I just can't!' Becky's voice was serious. I knew this whole secret Western stuff had really been bothering her. It would have bothered me, too, if Gary were my dad. It was weird that he'd kept part of his life from her, especially part of his horsy life. Even more especially since he was trying to prepare all of us for our first Western Show. It didn't make sense. 'Anyway, Jenna's coming soon. Can't she help you with this creep?'

'Jenna's not coming for weeks and Nicki's only staying one night. She'll be back at St Mary's Ladies College by then making sure her photo's in the school online newsletter.'

'Ash? Western?'

'Knock yourself out,' I grumbled. We hung up and I glared at the phone for a while, hoping that this was all just a bad dream. That I'd wake up to find that Dad was at work at the hospital, Honey and

Toffee were in the stable, and Miller Lodge was entirely a figment of my imagination.

'Ashleigh Miller! Ashleigh Miller!'

It was time for a reality pill. A big huge sharp one that gets stuck in your throat and you just can't choke down no matter how much elixir of misery you drink.

I stuck my head through the kitchen door and peered into the hall. 'What do you want?'

Nicki King sucked in her breath, her hands on her hips. 'That's no way to talk to a paying guest. Any more of that and I might have to complain to the manager.'

I coughed, a little louder than I needed to. 'What can I do for you?'

'I want my horse fed and watered and I want his rug changed and I want that poky box you call a stable mucked out. I'm riding in a show tomorrow and I don't need manure stains on his socks. And make sure his tail bag is secure and I don't want him in a halter overnight.' Nicki managed all of this in one breath.

'That's quite a list,' I said, anger rising in me like a pot boiling over on the stove. 'Maybe you'd get to know your horses better if you took care of them yourself. It's called bonding. If you could be bothered to bond with them, maybe then you wouldn't keep getting rid of them.'

Nicki's face grew red and tight. 'How dare you! You wait until my parents find out what you said. You just wait.'

Nicki turned and stomped up the stairs. I heard a door slam and muffled voices.

Who cares? I thought. I can't stand Nicki. I never could.

But the truth was I did care. I didn't like Nicki or want to be friends with her. I particularly didn't want to be her stablehand, or her slave for that matter. But I loved Mum and Dad and I wanted their B & B to be a big success. So if that meant putting up with Nicki King for one night I supposed that was just what I had to do.

Feet marched down the stairs and I closed the kitchen door quickly, hiding behind it, holding my breath. On the other side of the door, Nicki was whining loudly to her father, who assured her that 'that girl' would never get away with answering back to her.

The front desk bell rang over and over. First I heard Mum's voice, then Dad's. Then Jason's. All the arguing had woken him up.

'Ashleigh Louise! Come here this instant!'

It was only a matter of time. I took a deep breath then slunk into the hall. Mum was red, Dad was white, Jason was wild-eyed and screeching. Mr King was all three at once. Only Nicki looked pleased.

Ten minutes later I was apologizing to Nicki. Two minutes after that I was hosing out her float. Ten minutes later I was in the stable, mucking out her horse's poo and swapping his travel rug for a polar fleece combo.

It was late when I finally fell into bed, exhausted. I could hear Nicki whining at her parents, stomping from room to room and complaining that the television in the guest lounge wasn't big enough, clear enough or good enough, and there was no pay TV, only stock reports and the community station.

Suffer, Nicki, I thought as sleep claimed me. I couldn't wait until checkout time tomorrow morning. It was one thing to have been at South Beach Stables with her, but to live with her was the closest I'd come to sleeping on a bed of nails.

Next morning I woke to the sound of loud and angry voices. I had a quick, just-woken-up think and prayed that my parents hadn't gone temporarily insane and were begging the Kings not to leave.

I pulled my dressing gown on and shoved my feet into my slippers, then slipped as quietly as I could down the stairs.

I stuck my head around the corner at the bottom of the stairs. Mr King was shouting at my parents, Nicki and her mother were standing behind him with their arms folded. Nicki was wearing a very satisfied look on her face.

'I refuse absolutely to pay this bill,' Mr King bellowed, his face flushing red and becoming darker with each word he said. 'I specifically requested a five o'clock wake-up and for breakfast to be served by five-thirty. It's now eight twenty-three and we're still here, no breakfast has been prepared for us and Prince remains in that cardboard box you have the hide to call a stable when he should be in the float and halfway to Winmollong by now!'

When he finished, his face was the colour of a ripe passion fruit.

Mum turned and looked at me. Dad looked at me. Nicki and her mother and the Human Passion Fruit glared at me.

'What?' I said, smoothing down my hair and stepping into the hall. It was bad enough having to face all these angry people in my dressing gown without having just-woken-up clown hair as well. 'What did I do?'

'It's what you didn't do, Ash,' Mum said. Her lips were thin. 'You were supposed to have Nicki's horse ready to go two hours ago.'

I couldn't believe it. The only reason I'd overslept in the first place was Nicki-related exhaustion.

'Why can't she look after her own horse?' I cried. 'If she could just have been bothered to do it herself none of this would have happened.'

Mr King slammed his hand down on the front desk. 'I've had enough of this. The service here has been nothing but incompetent and my daughter has been treated in a despicable manner. I will personally report this establishment to the National Hotels Association.'

Dad's face went white.

'Can we offer you a complimentary overnight stay on your way back home?' Mum said, trying to smile.

'You most definitely can not,' Mr King roared. 'And this is what I think of your account!' He picked up the yellow piece of paper I knew to be the bill, tore it up and then threw the pieces on the floor. 'Nicki, Priscilla, we're leaving.'

'But, Dad! Someone has to load Prince for me,' Nicki wailed.

Mr King's face puffed up and his eyes stuck out. He was purple again. The vein on the side of his neck was throbbing. 'DO IT YOURSELF!'

Nicki's mouth fell open. She opened and closed it a few times then fixed her eyes on me. 'I'll never forgive you for this, Ashleigh Miller. Never!'

The Kings marched from the foyer, slammed the door and were gone.

Good riddance, I thought.

I turned to go back up the stairs. It was time to get dressed, feed my horses and get ready for Riding Club. It was one of our last training days before the Western Show and I needed as much practice as I could get.

'Where do you think you're going?'

I turned back to my parents. 'Upstairs to get ready for Riding Club.'

Dad shook his head. 'No fear, Ash.'

I looked at Mum. 'What's going on?'

Mum sighed. 'Ashleigh, we've had enough. It was only a small thing you were asked to do. Just to take care of that horse for one night. Now they've gone without paying their bill and we're out of pocket.'

'We won't be for long,' Dad grumbled. 'You're going to pay us back out of Horse Cents. And you're grounded from Riding Club, indefinitely.'

'No!' I cried. I could feel tears stinging my eyes. 'That's not fair. It's not my fault Nicki's a spoiled brat!'

'It's not your fault,' Dad said. 'But you let us down, Ash. Have you forgotten it was your idea to offer stabling in the first place?'

'Your father and I are clueless when it comes to horses,' Mum added. She sat down in her chair and buried her face in her hands. I didn't know if she was crying or just very tired.

They were right. They were totally right. Nicki had been making my life a misery, but her parents had done the same thing to Mum and Dad. The least I could have done was get Prince loaded. That way the Kings would have been out of our lives sooner and Mum and Dad would have been paid.

'I'm sorry,' I said. 'But do I have to pay you? Do I have to miss Riding Club?'

'Yes and yes,' Dad said. 'It seems to us that the only things that mean anything to you are horses and money. So until you learn to be responsible, that's just the way it has to be.'

'It's not fair!' I yelled again. 'You're mean. You hate me, don't you?'

'Of course not,' Mum said. 'We love you more than anything.'

'Not more than Jason,' I sobbed. I rubbed at my nose with my sleeve. 'Not more than the B & B.'

'Ash, that's enough.' Dad turned his back to me and headed for the kitchen.

What? Was he just going to ignore me?

'I'm running away!' I said. 'Then you'll be sorry.'

'See you at dinner,' Mum said. She sat at the computer at the reception desk and tapped the mouse.

I couldn't believe it. They were both doing it. It was almost like they'd planned it. I turned and ran up the stairs into my room, stomping as hard as I could then slammed the door so violently the windows rattled. Jason started crying then. Good! I thought. Let them suffer the way they're making me suffer.

I threw myself down on the bed and cried. I couldn't go to Riding Club and I had to give away my hard-earned Horse Cents money.

My life was over.

twelve

Saddle Up!

'Who can tell me what this is?' Gary Cho smiled at the Shady Creek riders.

Carly raised her hand. I nudged Becky gently in the ribs, grinning. It had been reasonably easy to persuade Dad to let me come back to Riding Club. Sure, he'd stuck to his guns and I'd missed that last meeting, but a fifty dollar donation (in other words, bribe) to the Cruel Parents United Fund, on top of the money owed by the Kings, from the now seriously depleted Horse Cents fund had softened him up. I was now allowed back at Riding Club. Thank goodness!

'It looks like a saddle, Gary,' Carly said. She turned to Flea and Ryan and rolled her eyes. They chuckled.

Gary patted the seat of the saddle that he'd gently placed on a portable saddle rack. We were seated in our outdoor classroom, a collection of upside down milk crates and logs under a tree. It was a sunny day, but I still preferred to snuggle inside my coat.

'Very insightful, Carly,' Gary said, beaming. 'Now, can anyone tell me anything else about this object, anything new?'

I raised my hand. 'It's a Western saddle.' It was a gorgeous tan colour, leather by the looks of it, and decorated with an amazing floral design in silver.

'Well done,' Gary said, flicking his dark eyes over Carly's face. She stared back at him, bold as usual. 'Can anyone name the parts of the Western saddle?'

'Isn't that handle thing at the front called the horn?'

'That's right, Jodie.' Gary rested his hand on the tall horn at the front of the saddle, where the pommel on an all-purpose saddle would go. 'What's it used for?'

'Holding on to!' Julie giggled.

'Not quite,' Gary said. 'Its traditional purpose is for holding the lariat. It was tied to the horn with rawhide. A cowboy—'

'Or girl!' I burst out.

Gary smiled. 'Or girl, could secure a cow to the horn as well. What else do you notice about the Western saddle?'

'The seat's so deep,' Becky mused.

'That's for comfort on all those long cowboy rides,' Gary said. 'It keeps the rider in a secure position as well.'

'How comfortable is it?' Becky looked her father clearly in the eye.

'Not sure,' Gary said. 'I've never used one.'

Becky's mouth dropped open. I gave her a look. First Gary had 'forgotten' his years as a Western rider, now he was lying about them. It didn't make any sense at all. Not to me or to Becky.

'The stirrups are weird,' Ryan said, pointing.

'Hey!' Flea puffed out his chest. As Shady Creek Riding Club's one and only experienced Western rider he wasn't going to take anyone insulting his sport.

'Not weird, Ryan,' Gary said. 'Just different. Wooden, actually. They're called ox-bows and are designed for long periods in the saddle. As is the raised cantle at the back of the seat.' Gary ran his hand down the saddle, from horn to cantle. 'It's much higher than your regular all-purpose.' Gary rested his hand on the horn.

'What are those strips of leather for?' Jodie called, pointing to four long tan strips that were sewn into the seat of the saddle.

Flea wriggled on his crate. 'They're for tying extra things to the saddle.'

'Spot on,' Gary said. 'Cowboys had to carry everything they needed with them in saddlebags. A bedroll was usually tied on top with baler twine.'

'What's with the stirrup leathers?' Becky scrutinized the saddle, a look of total concentration on her face.

Gary smiled. 'Western saddles have a fender rather than stirrup leathers, which protect the rider's legs. It's much wider, more of a flap than a leather, and as you can see, this one is very beautifully decorated. There's one more main diff—'

'The girth!' I cried. 'It's made of cord!'

'Right again, Ash. Except Western saddles have a cinch, not a girth, and this particular saddle is a Western Pleasure saddle so it has only one cinch attachment.' Gary lifted the fender and pointed.

'Have you learned all of this from a book, Dad?' Becky said suddenly. I sucked in my breath. I'd never heard her call him 'Dad' at Riding Club before. Never. Becky had always had to endure so much from the Creepketeers over what they saw as favouritism that she practically disowned him every meeting. Now she was calling him 'Dad'? This was serious.

My eyes flicked from Gary's face to Becky's and back again. It was one of those moments. I could tell, straight away, that he knew. He knew that she knew. He stared at Becky. She stared right back at him, waiting, hoping that he'd finally come clean.

I studied Gary's face. His cheeks flushed just a little but his gaze was strong. 'As a matter of fact, I have. Flea has been most helpful as well.'

Flea seemed to swell to at least twice his normal size. Well, his head did, anyway.

'But the photos, Dad, of you and that horse, and you were all dressed up like a cowboy and you were a champion.' The words gushed from Becky's mouth like she had no control over them.

Gary turned pale. Everyone sat silently, staring at Gary. I grabbed for Becky's hand and squeezed it.

'Dad?' Becky's eyes were wide and brimming with tears.

'I-I ...' Gary stammered. 'Sorry, Becky. I just ...'

It was horrible. The whole of Riding Club was holding its breath. I held on tight to my best friend's hand.

'Gary, can you tell us about the bridle?'

I never expected to be grateful to Flea for anything. But right at that moment, I could have kissed him.

Gary held up a tan-coloured leather and silver bridle with a very unusual bit attached. He looked at it for a few minutes, as if he couldn't remember what it was.

'Dad, the bridle?' Becky said softly.

'The bridle,' Gary said. He cleared his throat and the colour returned to his face. 'Yes, the bridle. In some ways the Western bridle is a lot like the English bridle. But as you can see there's no noseband—'

'How pretty!' Julie cried. 'Why don't our bridles have silver on them?'

'Most of our bridles are plain snaffle bridles,' I said. 'We use them because they suit so many different types of riding.'

'Like our all-purpose saddles,' Becky said, nodding.

'The silver is used for decoration,' Gary explained.

'It's 'cos we cowboys are so stylish.' Flea grinned, turning to us all.

Gary coughed. 'Ahem. Western bridles like this one are often called "one-ear" or "split-ear" bridles. See how the headpiece has been made from a single piece of leather? It has slits cut into it which fit around each of the horse's ears.'

'What for?' Ryan said, scratching his head. I've noticed something about Ryan. Whenever he thinks he gets an itchy scalp.

'It's to prevent the bridle being pulled off accidentally,' Gary explained.

'Tell us about the bit,' Jodie said.

Gary smiled. 'This is a Western curb bit. It has no joint so it looks a bit nasty when you hold it up against, say, your eggbutt snaffle, but Western horses are ridden with such light contact with the mouth that it's really not harsh at all. And most Western bits are made from sweet iron. As it rusts it gets sweeter, which encourages a horse to salivate. But at the end of the day Western riding is all about the seat and legs, not the rider's contact with the horse's mouth. A Western horse is traditionally ridden with just the weight of the rein maintaining contact with the mouth.'

'I heard Western riders use hackamores,' Sandra said, waving her hand in the air. 'Is that true?'

'What's a hackamore?' I was out of my depth now.

'It's a bitless bridle,' Becky said. 'They work by putting pressure on the horse's nose, poll and curb groove. Their chin, really.'

'Will we get to use them?' I asked. I wanted to be a real Western rider.

Gary shook his head. 'Hackamores have no contact with the mouth but in inexperienced hands they can be very severe. Sorry, Ash. Honey will be very happy with her usual bit.'

'What about the saddle blanket?' Flea said. 'You haven't talked about that yet.'

'Thanks for the reminder.' Gary reached into his crate and pulled out a thick saddle blanket with dark blue and orange stripes and black tassels.

'Wow,' Jodie said. 'That's heaps nicer than our Riding Club saddlecloths. Why can't we get those?'

Gary held up the saddle blanket and we all 'oohed'. (All except Carly, who yawned as wide and loud as a hippo.) 'The Western saddle blanket is usually bright and decorated. It's made of heavy wool, which absorbs the horse's sweat. The whole idea of a blanket like this is to prevent chafing and sores. For the horse, not the rider.'

Gary excused himself and returned a few minutes later with Bonnie, his huge Pinto mare. Becky looked desperate.

'Flea, get up here and tack her up for me, mate.'

'Can't you show us?' Becky called.

Gary shook his head, composed. 'Not now, Beck.'

Becky exhaled sharply and shook her head. I could tell there was going to be a very serious conversation in the Cho house later that day. Whether Becky would get the answers she was looking for was another issue.

Flea ran a body brush over Bonnie's back and under her belly, making sure there were no clumps of mud or prickles on her coat that could pinch her under the saddle. Then he folded a large, soft towel in half and, standing on Bonnie's near, or left side, placed it gently on her back. I'd noticed that since Gary had started relying on him so much he'd changed. He was becoming helpful. He was proud of what he knew and prouder still of being asked to share it. He was almost becoming normal.

'For the dirt,' Flea explained when Sandra asked about the towel. 'Your Western saddle blanket doesn't come cheap. The towel protects it from dirt and sweat.'

Gary laughed. 'To an extent.'

I glanced quickly at Becky but her mask didn't flicker.

Flea laid the gorgeous saddle blanket down on top of the towel and then lifted the saddle from the rack. It looked heavy but he lifted it without so much as a groan. He laid it down on the saddle blanket and flicked the cinch over the saddle. It hung from the saddle on Bonnie's offside.

Flea reached under Bonnie's belly for the cinch and, lifting the fender aside, fed the cinch through the buckle, wrenching it up and securing it. Bonnie swung her head around and rested her gentle brown eyes on Flea. Gary stroked her nose.

'Did we get that, everyone?' Gary said.

The Shady Creek riders nodded, spellbound. Flea bridled Bonnie and in no time she stood before us, a fully decked-out Pinto looking every bit the Western horse.

'Who wants a Western lesson?' Gary said.

We cheered. We were ready for anything.

Gary split us into groups and we rotated training sessions for the rest of the day. I only managed to trip myself, rather than the judge as well, in the Showmanship lesson. And I showed everyone in my Halter Class lesson a tail braid that would have made a hairdresser weep with envy. In the Hunter Under Saddle session (Western dressage) I got into trouble (which spells arena muck-out) for 'whoo-hooing' when Honey took three steps backwards on my command. But no matter what I did or how hard I listened to Flea, Honey wouldn't come to the party. It was head up high and trot all the way.

'Guess you can't teach an old mule new tricks,' Carly said, leering. It was one thing to hate me. That I could handle. But hate my horse?

'No, you can't,' I snapped. 'Which is why I'm surprised you are even entering in the show, especially after your last competition. How do you spell "disqualified" again?'

'C-A-R-L,' Becky began.

'Just shut up, Rebecca's Garden,' Carly bellowed.

Becky's face grew red. 'I'm sick of you. If you hate Riding Club so much why don't you just leave. Do us all a favour—'

'No way,' Carly said, her lips twisted into a sick, creepy smile, and nothing but venom in her eyes. 'I'd rather be branded than leave.'

'But why?' Becky wailed.

Carly's eyes narrowed like a snake's. 'If I left Riding Club you'd be happy. I don't want you to be happy. Ever.'

'You *creep!*' Becky gasped.

'Beck!' I hissed.

She swung around. 'What?'

I jerked my head in the direction of the warm-up arena. Becky gasped. Gary was riding Bonnie. He wasn't just riding, he was loping. I recognised the light, swinging canter Flea had demonstrated at an earlier lesson.

'What's going on?' I said.

Becky shook her head. 'I just don't know. But I can't take it any more. If it's the last thing I ever do, I'm gonna find out.'

thirteen

Missing in Action

'I'm not sure I want to sign it. I don't even want to go any more. I'll just go to the high school in town with Becky. Forget you ever heard the name "Linley Heights School"!'

Mum pushed the scholarship entrance exam form in front of me. I buried my face in my hands.

'What is it, Ash?'

I shook my head. 'I don't know. I wanted to go. At first. But now—'

'Becky?' Mum watched me intently. Jason grabbed hold of a handful of her hair, yanked and screeched with delight.

I nodded, swallowing hard. There was something sticky in my throat, like I'd rammed a big chunk of bread into my mouth and was trying to choke it down. 'And the rest.'

Mum waved the cheque for the exam fee. Jason reached out his fat little fingers for it, his eyes wide and determined. 'It's okay. We want you to go.'

'You want me to go?' I was shocked. I thought they'd be crying, screaming, begging me not to leave their nest. But here was my mother pushing a cheque at me, practically throwing me out into the wide cruel world.

'It's a great chance, Ash,' Mum said. Her eyes were wistful. 'With that scholarship, you can get the kind of education at Linley that your father and I could never afford. And riding is your ticket.'

'I'll get just as good an education in town,' I said. I pushed the form back across the kitchen table. 'And besides, if you want me to leave home so badly why can't I just live with Jenna? I could go to high school with her. I wouldn't be alone then.'

Mum pushed the form back again. 'You won't be alone. You'll have Honey. Now sign.'

I looked into her eyes. 'I'm scared, Mum. I'm just so scared.'

Mum smiled. 'You? Ashleigh Miller? I've never

believed that the word "scared" was even in your vocabulary.'

'What if I hate it? What if I stink at Linley and everyone else is a better rider than me? What if I don't make any friends?'

'You haven't been accepted yet. What say we worry about your list when and if it happens? Eh?'

'Have we got that paw print on paper yet, Helen?' Dad swung into the kitchen wearing his favourite apron and a pair of heavy-duty pink rubber gloves. We'd just said goodbye to our latest overnight guest and it was his turn to scrub the bathroom, but by the look of him, you'd think he'd just spent a week at an island resort.

'Having fun, Dad?' I said.

'You bet! Who'd want to go back to the rat race?' Dad peeled off his gloves and hovered by the coffee maker.

'Rat race? You worked at Shady Creek and Districts Hospital.' I raised one eyebrow. 'What was ratty about that?'

'You'd better get this scholarship, Ash,' Dad said, pushing a button on the coffee machine. 'That fee is non-refundable.'

'Thanks for the support,' I said, grimacing. Sometimes I wondered about my parents. They were supposed to worship the ground I walked on. Being their precious firstborn and, for eleven whole years, their only child and all. But here was Dad more worried about a lousy scholarship exam fee than my emotional wellbeing. 'If that's how you feel I'll just sign. You've probably been upstairs measuring my room. I s'pose you're gonna turn it into another guest room?'

Dad slammed down his coffee cup hard. Coffee spilled out onto the bench. 'Ashleigh Louise, I am disgusted. How could you say such a thing?'

I swallowed and hung my head. I always overdid things. 'Sorry.'

'So you should be.' Dad picked up his cup again and raised it to his mouth. His eyes smiled out at me. 'We're turning it into a billiard room.'

'Dad!' I threw my pen at him. He bellowed and ripped the tea towel from the handle on the oven door and spun it around for a few moments. I knew what was coming and screamed. That was all it took. Dad drew the tea towel back and whipped it out again.

'Missed me!' Mum handed back the pen, and I

scribbled my signature on the paper then leapt from my seat.

'Just testing you. Now for the real thing!' Dad drew the towel back again and I braced myself, waiting for the sting. He flicked the towel at me and, missing again, sent the tissue box spinning across the table.

'You need some practice,' I yelled, dancing around the kitchen. Jason watched me with wide eyes, torn between laughing and crying.

'And I'm gonna get it!' Dad threw back his head and laughed. 'So run for your life!'

I screamed again and bolted out of the kitchen, throwing open the back door and leaping from the top step onto the path.

'I can't believe you fell for the oldest trick in the book! You're a funny kid, Ash,' Dad yelled after me.

'I'm off to work anyway,' I said. 'So I'll put my order in now for a nice hot yummy dinner when I get back.'

Dad laughed again. 'Your mum and I will be very happy with whatever you cook.'

This time I had to laugh.

I caught Honey (more like she caught me) and gave her a quick brush.

Once Honey was tacked up I set off in the direction of Shady Trails Riding Ranch. It was Saturday morning and I was on the verge of being late for work.

'I don't wanna ride.' Mikenzie McMurray had wrapped her long pink scarf around her neck so many times she looked to be in danger of suffocation. 'It's cold. I could catch pneumonia. Mother said I was never to be exposed to pneumonia.'

'You don't catch pneumonia,' Pree said, beaming. 'You develop it. When I was two I had it and it started as a throat infection with this really unbelievable fever and Mum said the fever just wouldn't go away for days and days and I chucked up all over the back seat of the car and then—'

'Thanks, Pree.' I held up my hand and Pree giggled and ran her thumb and forefinger across her lips, 'zip-it' style. She moved Jasmine into the lead horse position. Three kids on ponies wearing brightly coloured helmets lined up behind her.

'It's windy. And there are clouds overhead. Mother said I was never to go out in the rain.' Mikenzie tucked the tassels of the scarf inside the collar of her coat like she needed extra protection from Shady Creek's mild winter weather.

'It's not raining.' I scrutinized the sky. 'I don't reckon there's even a single chance of a single drop. Right, Pree?'

Pree saluted me. 'Too right, Ash. Shady Creek hasn't seen so much as a squirt for weeks and weeks. In fact, we should probably think about changing the name of the town to Shady Puddle. Hey, what d'you call a clean Appaloosa? Spotless! D'you get it? Spotless!'

Savannah moaned. Okay, so Pree's jokes weren't to everybody's taste but they were better than Gary's. 'Just get over it, Mikenzie. A proper bout of a real illness might actually make you interesting.'

'Don't tease me!' Mikenzie shrieked. Honey stiffened a little. I stroked her neck and murmured to her. 'Mother said you were never to tease me. She said that I was to call her immediately if you teased me.'

'Waa, waa, waa.' Savannah rubbed her eyes, fake-crying. I swallowed, hoping more than anything that Jason and I were destined for a better sibling relationship than the McMurray girls.

'We have a trail group waiting,' I said in as low a voice as I could manage. 'Are you two coming or not? Pree can't take the trail alone.'

'So you're saying that Priyanka isn't good enough to take us out on her own?' Savannah held her chin up and looked down at me from Penny's back. 'I believe it's your duty to inform the rest of the riders that we're being led by an incompetent.'

Pree twisted around in her saddle and gave us her best, most radiant smile. 'Any trail leader under sixteen has to have a second trail leader with them. It's the rule. Ask your Nanna.'

Savannah snorted. 'Ha! Back home I was a trail leader all by myself. I didn't need anyone to hold *my* hand. In fact, I should lead this group. Ha!'

'It's going to rain!' Mikenzie wailed. 'I felt a drop. I really did. There was a drop of rain.'

'Mikenzie, I promise you it will not rain. You won't get pneumonia and you're not allergic to horses.' I was practically begging her. We had a group of kids here whose parents had all paid for a two-hour trail ride. I couldn't let them down.

Mikenzie watched the sky suspiciously for a moment then nodded slowly.

I sighed, relieved, and asked Pree to head out. She was taking the lead. I was going to bring up the rear. It was the best way to make sure that nobody got in front of us and that no one was left behind. I'd learned that one of the problems with taking trail groups was that as trail leaders, we were usually meeting the riders for the first time, and so we had no way of knowing anything about their riding skills. I'd also learned that anybody from 'hotheads' who wanted nothing more than to gallop for hours to total equinophobes went horse riding.

Honey and I followed Penny and Savannah down the trail, nose to tail. I wanted to be as close as possible to the group, firstly for Pree's jokes (Why did the dirty horse cross the road twice? He was a dirty double crosser!), and secondly so I could listen out for any word of complaint from the McMurrays. I didn't want any nasty surprises on our return.

We came to the creek that ran down the back of Shady Trails. It was only knee deep on the horses, but it looked cold.

'Is this the famous Shady Creek?' Savannah said loudly. 'What exactly is a creek, anyway?'

'It's like a river,' I grumbled.

'This is a river?' Savannah stared at the creek, incredulous. 'Ha! At home we have real rivers. This is pathetic. Shady Creek is pathetic. Ha!'

Pree shook her feet from her stirrups and lifted them high. The first rider followed her, then the next and the next, splosh-splashing through the water and giggling all the way. Mikenzie was next. I was stuck behind Savannah, and craned my head to make sure everyone was across okay.

Bartok had stopped in the middle of the creek.

'Giddup, Bartok!' I shouted.

Mikenzie wailed, 'He won't move. I'll be stuck here in the middle of this lake forever and I'll probably get hypothermia. Or malaria. Mother said I was never to be exposed to hypothermia or malaria. If Mother knew I was here she'd—'

'Well, she's not,' Savannah snapped. 'So get out of the river.'

'I can't!' Mikenzie's voice was all cracked. Great, I thought. One more complaint about me and Pree to add to the McMurray girls' already very long list.

'Excuse me.' I squeezed Honey past Savannah, brushing against her leg.

'My Eurochampion chapettes!' she cried. 'If you've so much as wrinkled my Eurochampion chapettes, I'll make sure Nanna docks your pay.'

'Whatever,' I grumbled. I couldn't believe I'd actually wanted to meet the McMurray girls. I thought about sending an email to their mother describing the many dangers and diseases that Shady Creek had to offer. They'd be on the next plane home before you could say 'two spoiled brats'. The only thing that was stopping me was Mrs McMurray. She loved them so much and wanted their stay with her to be something they remembered forever.

I pulled Honey up alongside Mikenzie and tugged on the headpiece of Bartok's bridle. 'C'mon, buddy! Giddup.'

Bartok stared straight ahead. He wasn't usually stubborn. Maybe he was as sick of Mikenzie's whining as I was.

I tugged again. 'Go on! Get out of here.'

Bartok sniffed at, then pawed at the water with his offside (right) foreleg again and again. There was an incredible splosh, like someone had put a huge beater into the water. It splashed, it sprayed. Creek water soaked my joddies. Mikenzie screamed.

'Get them out of there, Ash!' Pree said. She knew what was coming. So did I.

'Get up, Bartok. Get up!' I tugged and tugged, but it was no use. In less than ten seconds Bartok was on his knees, then his side. And, with Mikenzie now crouched up on her feet, still clamped to his back and still screaming, Bartok rolled. Right there in the creek. Then he stood up and had a good shake as if nothing out of the ordinary had happened.

The trail riders stared. Pree stared. I stared. Savannah, for once, was speechless. It wasn't something you saw every day. A soaked and dripping Mikenzie was spitting out creek water, and balancing on the very top of the saddle like a cat on a fence! I was impressed.

'Wow,' Pree said. 'I've never seen anything like that in my whole entire life. Oh, except this one time at riding camp, this girl was riding a huge horse with an attitude problem and he did the same thing. Rolled with her on his back. Except that was in the arena. She was washing sand out of places she never knew she had for a week after that!'

Mikenzie blinked a few times. Water dripped from her helmet onto her nose and down her chin. Her clothes were drenched and her joddies were coated in mud. I wondered about her boots. They looked to be full to the brim. I wouldn't have been surprised to see fish swimming in them.

'Get me out of this *creek* and off this horse!' Mikenzie spoke like each word was hurting her.

I grabbed hold of Bartok's bridle again and just as I was about to give an almighty tug, Savannah charged towards me.

'Mikenzie, hang on.' Savannah reached up from her saddle and snapped a thin branch from a tree. She ripped the leaves away with one stroke of her gloved hand and brought the branch down hard on Bartok's rump.

The grey gelding flinched.

'No!' I cried. 'Don't hurt him.'

Savannah raised her hand, brandishing the stick. 'No horse does what he did to my sister and gets away with it.' She whacked him again. The pony jumped out of the creek. Mikenzie screamed.

'That's enough!' I cried. I leaned over in my saddle and made a grab for the stick.

Savannah held it high. 'That horse will be spending its last night at this riding school. You can count on that.'

She kicked Penny hard and the mare burst into a canter, sending icy cold water spraying over me. Mikenzie cantered after her.

'Wait!' Pree yelled.

'You don't know the way back! Stop!' I shouted.

But they were gone. Pree and I looked at each other.

'You stay with the trail riders and I'll go after them,' I said.

I gathered my reins.

The trail riders moved their horses out of my way and I cantered past them down the track. I'd ridden this trail dozens of times and knew where to turn and exactly where branches hung low over the track. But the McMurray girls didn't.

Honey cantered on and on but there was no sign of them. Figuring they must have found their way home, I pulled Honey up. She was sweaty, and I knew I needed to cool her out. We would have to walk back to the stables or risk having a sick horse. My mind was racing. How did the McMurray girls disappear so quickly? And Pree? Was she okay with the trail group? I couldn't turn back and help her now. I would have to tell Mrs Mac.

I made my way straight to the stables, but there was no sign of Penny or Bartok. Their stalls were empty and their saddle racks were bare. I began to worry. They'd had a few minutes head start and should have been back. Walking Honey back to the stables gave them at least another ten minutes on top of that head start. My tummy started to fizz. I untacked Honey and placed a light cotton rug on her back, which was wet with sweat. She needed to be warm and dry. I made sure she had a cool drink and a haynet to nibble on. She'd been cooled out enough to enjoy a small snack. I would never give her a huge meal straight after returning from a workout like that.

I left the stables and ran, passing Rachael who was pushing a wheelbarrow with a pitchfork and rake balanced on top of it.

'Have you seen Savannah and Mikenzie?' I said. I felt desperate.

Rachael shook her head. 'No, thank goodness. You know, they're driving me nuts. Only yesterday—'

'Thanks, Rachael!' I kept running, checking in every barn, every yard. They weren't in the kiosk or the party room or the shop. They weren't in the staff room either.

I felt sick. And once I saw Pree leading the trail group, who were all giggling (probably at another one of Pree's world-famous jokes), back into the holding yard, and I saw that Mikenzie and Savannah weren't with her, I felt even more sick.

I went straight to Mrs Mac's office. I couldn't delay telling her. As I put my hand onto the handle, I stopped and looked over my shoulder, hoping that they would be standing there, hoping this was some sort of cruel joke, hoping that any second now I would hear Savannah say, 'Ha! I win.'

fourteen

Search Party

'Ash, I can't believe I'm hearing this. I asked you to look after my girls and you've let me down over and over.' Mrs McMurray was furious. Her face was red and her blue eyes, usually so calm and kind, were flashing.

'But I—' I began. I wanted to tell her everything. About how none of this had been my fault and that Savannah had been out to get me from her first day in Shady Creek. Sure, I'd made up a dangerous reptile, and a tack-cleaning contest, but I hadn't trained Bartok to roll in the middle of a creek with a precious McMurray girl on his back. Mrs Mac held up her hands. 'I don't want to hear another word.

I'm calling the police and I want every staff member out looking for them.'

Mrs McMurray picked up the phone and dialled. She relayed the story to a police officer. The more she spoke the worse I felt. They *were* from overseas. They *were* homesick. They'd never been away from their mother before and their father was interstate on business. It was true. I'd let her down. Big time.

Just as Mrs McMurray hung up the phone, the door of her office burst open. Rachael Cho was standing in the doorway, panting and waving her hands in front of her face.

'They're back,' she gasped.

Mrs McMurray seemed to collapse a little. 'Thank goodness! Are they all right?'

Rachael shook her head. 'No, the horses are back. They've found their way home, but there's no sign of Savannah or Mikenzie.'

Mrs McMurray covered her mouth with her hands. Tears welled in her eyes. 'Should I ring my son? Oh, I don't know. I wish Harold was here. He'd know what to do.'

My throat grew tight. I felt worse than ever. I should have taken better care of them. What if they were hurt? There were no Shady Boas out there, but there were snakes. Becky had seen red-bellies heaps of times. There were spiders as well. Everyone in the Creek knew to tip out their riding boots in the morning in case a funnel-web or a redback had moved in overnight. What if the McMurray girls didn't know about our Australian snakes and spiders? What if they thought that Australia was all kangaroos and koalas?

Mrs McMurray wiped away her tears and looked me in the eye. 'You're coming with me, Ashleigh. I want you in the saddle in five minutes and waiting for me in the holding yard. Rach, will you tack up Clarence for me, please, love?'

'No worries, Mrs McMurray.' Rachael disappeared.

'But Hon—' I began.

Mrs McMurray held up her hand. 'No buts. Five minutes.'

I nodded. There was nothing else I could do.

I turned and left the office, running as fast as I could to the stables. I owed Mrs Mac to be out there looking for her girls. I mean, I'd tried to help them, I'd tried to stop them from taking off and I'd gone after them. But I should have tried harder to be their friend. I felt awful, and all knotted inside, like I'd done something really bad and everybody knew about it. Something I was too ashamed to talk about with anyone.

But I was torn. Honey had been ridden hard, cooled out, fed and watered. I couldn't ride her for at least another forty-five minutes. As for Penny and Bartok, Sam had caught them and was sponging Penny down while Azz led Bartok in slow circles. I couldn't ride them. Pree had untacked Jasmine and vanished, most likely to fetch her a snack. But Jazz was so slow anyway, it'd be faster to go on foot. There was only one option.

Cassata.

Rachael had ridden her over in the morning. She never used her during the day, preferring Hector or Ajax, a new Quarter Horse gelding who'd arrived at the Ranch a few weeks earlier.

Cassata was standing patiently in her stall. She nickered when she saw me, and poked her sweet head over the stall.

'Am I glad to see you!' I let myself into her stall and ran my hand over her flanks. She was dry. Her haynet was long empty. She'd allow another rider, or even two, on her back besides me. She was the perfect choice.

I let myself out again, grabbed her tack from the

tack room, sent a prayer to the horse gods that Rachael would never know what I'd done (she may be a colleague, but as her little sister's best friend I'm always going to be a huge pain in the butt to her). I tacked up Cassata, stretched her legs and led her to the holding yard, just as Mrs McMurray was mounting Clarence.

Either she hadn't noticed that I was suddenly riding an Appaloosa with a dark brown face, neck and legs and a white rump covered in brown spots, or the fact that I was mounted on someone else's horse didn't matter to her just as long as I was on one.

Mrs Mac and I set off out of the holding yard in the direction of the trail. She had left the responsibility of the Ranch and the police in Sam's hands. We rode together for two hours, searching along the trail and into the bush. Mrs McMurray didn't speak the whole time, except to call out the girls' names and murmur a prayer. Cassata was the smooth and willing ride she had always been but she felt different. Strange. Rounder somehow. Figuring that she had probably put on some weight, I pushed it to the back of my mind.

It grew dark. Mrs McMurray gave me a look.

'We'll have to head back,' she said. 'Ash, there's something you have to know. I hold you responsible. You and Pree. As far as I'm concerned today is your last day at Shady Trails. I'll pay you what you're owed but then I'd appreciate it if you leave.'

'But Mrs—'

Mrs McMurray held up her hand, shaking her head slowly. 'I'm sorry. But I don't want to talk about it any more.'

She pulled Clarence in the direction of the Ranch. I sat mounted on Cassata, not quite ready to believe what I'd just heard. I was the first girl she'd put on at the Ranch besides Sam. I'd nearly lost Becky over my decision to work here. I'd taken care of her horses like they were mine. I touched the horse pendant she'd given to me instead of her granddaughters and felt the first hot tears run down my face. If I couldn't work at Shady Trails, I didn't know what I would do. I'd done every odd job, washed every car and made ribbon browbands to sell until my fingers ached, but Shady Trails was the best job, and one of the best times, I'd ever had.

'Please!' I called after her, sobbing. 'Don't do this. I tried to stop them, I-I …' I wiped at my tears with the back of my hand. 'Ask anyone who was on that ride.'

I racked my brain, trying to think through the fog.

Mrs McMurray pulled up and twisted around in the saddle.

I urged Cassata into a walk. She shook her head, but moved off after a gentle squeeze of my heels.

I joined Mrs Mac and looked into her eyes.

'Ash, I see my girls once every year or two. This is the first time they've ever come to visit me in Australia. My daughter-in-law was convinced that I couldn't manage at my ... well ... at my age. All I had to do was keep them safe and well for eight weeks. I brought up two boys of my own, but I needed to show her I could do it. That they were safe with me.' Mrs McMurray sighed and shook her head. 'She'll never let them stay with me again.'

'I'm sorry.' I held out my hand and Mrs Mac grabbed it, squeezing my fingers.

'I'm sorry, too.' Mrs McMurray closed her eyes, like she couldn't bear to see mine. 'But I still have to let you go.'

I gulped, just like Jason after a good cry. 'B-But what about Pree? She didn't go after them because I told her not to. I told her to stay with the trail riders.'

Mrs McMurray nodded slowly. 'Thanks for being honest, Ash. Pree's job here is safe. She's found a good friend in you. So have I, love.'

'Then why—' I cried.

Mrs McMurray shook her head again. 'One day you'll understand.'

My chest hurt. My head hurt. I was so angry, so frustrated. Why do grown-ups always say that? Why do they think I won't understand? I understand just fine.

'And, Ash, good luck with Linley Heights. I hope you make it.'

I pulled away from Mrs Mac and urged Cassata into a canter down the trail in the half-light. If I knew Rachael, I knew she'd be screaming by now and I would be even higher on her blacklist.

It wasn't long before the Ranch came into view. It was all lit up. There was a police car in the driveway outside Mrs Mac's office and, strangely, a taxi.

I slowed Cassata to a trot. I could see Rachael, her arms crossed and looking like she'd been sucking on hot chilli peppers.

'What gives you the right to just take off on my horse?'

I pulled Cassata up, slid to the ground and threw Rachael the reins. 'I'm sorry, okay. I'm sorry. Why is it always me that has to say sorry? Why am I always the one to blame?'

When she saw my tear-stained face, Rachael held up her hands. 'Relax, it's fine.'

She ran her hands down Cassata's legs, feeling for bumps or injuries. I left her to it and ran towards the stables. Honey was waiting. She nickered when she saw me. I let myself into her stall and threw my arms around her neck, the tears coming again. It was so unfair.

I felt a hand on my shoulder and turned around. Pree was leaning on the wall of Honey's stall, her long thick black plait hanging over her shoulder to her tummy. 'You okay?'

I shook my head and told her everything that Mrs Mac had said.

'Are you sure you heard her right?' Pree's dark eyes were wide with shock.

I nodded. 'You bet I did.'

I quickly ran a body brush over Honey's coat. It was completely dark now and I was afraid. My heart beat a little faster than usual as I thought about the ride home in the dark, down the road and through the bush trail, and the less than pleased parental greeting that was surely waiting for me.

'Maybe she didn't really mean it,' Pree said, hopefully. 'I'll explain everything that happened in the morning and maybe she'll change her mind.'

I sighed and shook my head, unable to speak. Pree's eyes brimmed with tears. I'd never seen her upset before.

Just as I ran into the tack room to fetch my saddle and bridle, I heard a voice.

'Ashleigh, are you here?' Rachael Cho was standing in the stable aisle. 'Dad's here with the float. He said we're taking you home.'

I wanted to collapse with relief. I emerged from the tack room. Pree scooped my gear from my arms.

'What about you?' I looked at Pree. My voice was tight.

'Jazz is staying the night. Mum's already waiting in the car park.' Pree bit at her bottom lip. 'Ash, I'm really sorry.'

I slipped Honey's halter over her nose and buckled it at her cheek, then clipped the lead rope to the ring under her chin.

'It's not your fault.'

'But I'll miss you, Ash.' Pree shook her head.

'No, I can't work here without you. I'm gonna tell Mrs Mac I quit.'

'No!' I said. I opened the stall door and tugged gently on Honey's lead rope. She took a careful step out of the stall. 'I want you to stay.'

Tears spilled down Pree's face. 'I'd hug you, Ash. But I'd drop your saddle!'

I led Honey from the Shady Trails stable complex for the very last time, stopping to take it all in, to commit every sight, sound and smell of the Ranch to memory.

I could see Gary's car and the Cho's float under the lights. Cassata was already loaded. Sam and Azz hovered by the ramp. I led Honey to the float, lifted my chin and walked her up the ramp. Azz closed the gate and then the ramp, sliding the bolts into place. I let myself out of the side door of the float and Sam ran at me, wrapping her arms around me.

'Wow,' I said. 'News sure does travel fast around here.'

'It's not right. It's just not right.' She sniffled and turned away. Azz put his arm around her. I shook his hand.

'Bit formal, Ash,' he teased.

I high-fived him instead.

I noticed a flickering in the office window and jerked around just in time to see a blonde head duck out of sight.

'Was that—'

Pree nodded. 'They're fine. They let the horses go, went for a walk into town and took a taxi back. I didn't know how to tell you.'

I was filled with anger. They were fine. I'd still lost my job, but they were fine.

I gave Pree a quick hug and climbed into the Chos' car. Gary leaned over the seat and smiled. 'You okay?'

I tucked my hair behind my ears. 'Yep.'

But I wasn't.

I felt just like I had when Jenna and I had busted up as best friends after my move to Shady Creek.

It was like a part of my life had died and nothing could ever bring it back.

fifteen

Wild Wild West

Without Shady Trails in my life I didn't know what to do with myself. Oh, sure, there were still two horses to look after, bed-and-breakfast duties, a baby brother and a Western Show to prepare for to help fill my day, but no matter what I did, Saturdays just seemed wrong.

Mum and Dad had no trouble finding plenty for me to do. The B & B was getting bookings every weekend and even some mid-week. I'd come down to breakfast in the morning (which I always had to make myself now that I was behind the guests, the baby and the horses in the pecking order) and find a nice long list of chores sitting neatly at my place at the table. Rather than understanding my despair at the loss of Shady Trails and having to hand in my uniform, my parents were thrilled to have an extra pair of hands who had no choice but to do the jobs or see Horse Cents completely depleted.

I focussed on the one thing that I knew would keep me sane: Jenna. She would be here soon! The weekend after the Western show, in fact. I couldn't wait to see her. By the time she arrived for the school holiday break, it would be a whole nine months since I'd seen her last. Nine months! That is a very long time to go without one of your best friends.

'This gear is so cool!' I said, wriggling into a purple long-sleeved shirt with huge silver buttons, a pointy silver collar and sequins. Becky, Pree and I were getting changed inside the Cho's float. It was Pinebark Ridge Western Riding Club Show Day and we were almost dressed to thrill.

Over the last few weeks we had trained non-stop in our spare time, had taken lessons from Flea in Western-style show grooming and dressing, and read every Western riding book we could get our hands on. We'd pored over the show program, carefully choosing which events we were going to have a go at, spent hours deciding how we were going to wear our hair under our cowgirl hats, and now we were really here!

Our horses were as beautiful as ever. They were all nibbling at haynets under the watchful eyes of our parents. All except Gary, that is. He'd made some excuse about having a sore back from lifting a box at the restaurant and had stayed at home on the lounge. I knew Becky well enough to know when she didn't want to talk and this was one of those times.

I did up the buttons, tucked the shirt inside my blue jeans and hooked my thumbs around my belt. 'Do I look like a cowgirl?'

'Do I look like one, too?' Becky looked amazing in a long-sleeved white shirt with tassels and gold sequins. She settled a white Western-style straw hat on her head. 'Yee-haa!'

'What about me?' Pree was wearing blue jeans with real, full-length chaps, brown boots and a red shirt that sparkled when she moved. The colour was the perfect match for her long black hair.

'Cowgirls or not, we all look hot,' I said. 'It was so awesome of Mrs Flea to lend us this stuff, eh?' Mum was going mental about where to hire Western gear. She didn't want me to buy it for just one day.

Mrs Fowler, Flea's mum, had opened her heart and her Western collection to the entire club. She'd ridden and competed in Western events since she was a kid and had never thrown any of her things away. She'd even lent us her collection of soft leather Western show halters, all decorated with gorgeous sterling silver. I just didn't understand how a person as decent as Mrs Fowler could have produced a kid like Flea.

'I get the feeling you might need your own Western gear, you like it so much.' Becky pulled at her pigtails, making sure they sat evenly under her hat.

'There's still so much to learn,' I said, sighing. 'I watched a DVD last night from America and this guy was riding and his horse was doing sliding stops and was spinning on the spot. He made it look so easy, but I bet it took years of practice.'

'Patience, my good friend,' Pree said, fiddling with her tie. 'Stop me if you've heard this one. Why did the cowboy ride his horse? Cos it was too heavy to carry. D'you get it? Too heavy to carry!'

'Now this,' Becky said, holding up a thick brown leather belt with a huge silver buckle, 'was Dad's. He doesn't know I've got it.'

Becky threaded the belt through the loops in her jeans and her outfit was complete. 'Well, girls? Are we ready to rock?'

'Are we ready to bootscoot?' I clapped my hands.

'You betcha!' Pree sang.

We were ready for anything.

It was eight-thirty on the dot and the show was about to open. I'd never been to the Pinebark Ridge Western Riding Club grounds, but I liked it already. There was one huge undercover arena with a grandstand, two warm-up areas, loads of float parking and a long row of stables available for hire on show days. Our first event was a Halter Class and as Honey, Charlie and Jasmine weren't Western breeds, like Appaloosas and Quarter Horses, they had been entered in the Other Breeds categories. It would be at least an hour before we'd be called and, with our horses safe, sound and happy with their haynets, we wanted to watch as much as we could of our first-ever Western Show. Becky, Pree and I settled ourselves in the grandstand, giggling as country music twanged and crackled through the rusty loudspeakers.

I'd never seen anything like it before. Officials wore Stetson hats and spangles. The place was thick with Appaloosas and Paint Horses. Riders and handlers, dressed in the most spectacular Western gear, prepared for a class called Open Halter Under Two Years Futurity. I was lost. It was like a completely new world.

'Whaddya reckon futurity is, eh, Beck?'

'It's like the Olympics of Western showing. There's big prize money up for grabs, but only the cream of the crop compete.' Becky looked bashful. 'I read about it in Dad's books.'

'Feel like talking about it?' I said as casually as I could.

Becky frowned. 'Why didn't he come? He never misses a show, especially not one I'm in. I just don't get it.'

'I just don't get why you haven't come straight out and asked him,' Pree said, raising her eyebrows.

Becky sighed. 'I have. So many times. But he just changes the subject or remembers something urgent that needs to be done at the restaurant or ...'

I patted Becky's knee. 'Don't stress. I reckon he'll tell you everything when he's ready.'

'S'pose,' Becky said. She folded her arms, crossed her legs and jiggled her foot.

A marshal standing at the arena gate shouted out

the next few classes and herded horses and handlers inside. The Quarter Horses were called and a particularly dashing young handler in a black hat led a stunning bay gelding into the arena.

'Call me totally sick, but is that Flea?' Becky squinted at him.

'It can't be,' I said, shivering. 'It goes against the laws of nature. That guy looks good. It can't be Flea.'

But it was. I didn't know who the gelding was or who he belonged to, but Flea turned in an amazing performance and won first place in the Gelding Two and Three Years Class. He was called back for the Champion and Reserve Quarter Horse Gelding Class and he won that as well. I was staring so hard at Flea and the horse with the triple-toned ribbon around his neck I thought my eyes were going to pop out of their sockets.

We sat and watched the rest of the Quarter Horses, then the Paint Horses and Solid Paint. Once the Appaloosas were called we knew it was time to get ready. The only things that stood between us and the Other Breeds were the Palouse Ponies.

Suddenly my heart gave a leap as I spotted two girls with whiny, twisted faces and large mouths.

One was tall and blonde, the other, shorter with dark hair.

'What are they doing here?' I spat. As far as I was concerned they were the reason I'd lost my job at Shady Trails. I didn't ever want to see them again. Much less at my first-ever Western Show. 'They've got no right to be here after what they did to me. I wish they'd just get lost.'

I felt mean. But anger does strange things to your mouth. It makes it open and lets horrible words tumble out of it one after the other.

'Again!' Pree said.

'They probably came to look down on everyone,' Becky said, glaring.

I pulled my cowgirl hat low over my eyes. 'As long as they don't recognise me.'

'They won't,' Pree said, patting my knee. 'You look amazing.'

My mouth fell open. 'Don't I always?'

Pree clapped her hand over her mouth. 'I didn't mean—'

I laughed and wrapped my arm around her shoulder. 'But I did!'

We scuttled back to our horses. I was tingling with nerves. I'd done dozens of shows, maybe more, but the feeling never went away — the butterflies, the fizziness. I hoped it never would. It kept me on my toes. It kept me fresh and alert and loving every single minute of it all.

'Here goes,' I murmured as I slipped the borrowed leather halter over Honey's sweet chestnut nose and tucked the headpiece behind her ears, pulling her forelock clear. The halter was gorgeous, a rich dark brown leather, decorated with engraved silver on the noseband and cheekpieces. The buckles were elaborate and made from silver with engravings of floral designs.

I threaded the chain of the lead rope under Honey's chin, clipping it just above the halter's offside cheekpiece. Clipping it there would give me more control than simply clipping it under her chin. As a complete Western rookie, I needed as much control in the arena as I could muster. The chain made up only about 40 centimetres of the lead rope, the rest was leather — dark chocolate brown and soft as skin. How I used the chain was very important. I could touch it in the Halter Class, but wasn't allowed to even brush against it with my fingertips in Showmanship.

Once I'd buckled the halter I stood back a few steps to admire Honey. She looked gorgeous. I had groomed her to perfection, scrubbing her white socks and the white blaze on her face until they glowed. Just as before any show, she had been shampooed, sweat-scraped and rubbed dry. I had groomed her again that morning, painted her feet with shiny black hoof oil and rubbed petroleum jelly around her eyes and nose to make them shine. I had brushed her mane and tail, and then decorated her mane by dividing it into almost twenty small bunches and simply twisting an elastic band around them, just the way Flea had shown us. She looked so perfect. My heart swelled with love and pride.

I held the lead rope tight in my right hand and brushed away some dirt from my jeans with my left. I patted the top of my head to make sure my white straw hat was in place and took a deep breath. It was show time.

Becky, Pree and I gathered by the arena gate with our horses, waiting to be called into the arena for the Other Breeds Led (Halter) Class. It wasn't long before a familiar redhead leading a sweet-faced white mare joined us.

'I can't believe they accepted your sack of dog meat in Other Breeds, Spiller,' Carly sneered. 'Either the show secretary's blind or doesn't know a mule when he sees one.'

I wanted to grab a huge handful of the nearest pile of horse poo I could find and smear it all over her emerald-green shirt. The only thing that was holding me back was the fact that I knew the shirt had come from the Mrs Fowler Western Gear Lending Service. Carly's sharp face hadn't though. My eyes flicked towards the arena. The last of the Palouse Ponies was being inspected by the judge. Surely there was enough time to rub a doover or two across Carly's cheeks.

In a split second the Champion and Reserve of the Palouse Ponies Class was announced. The pint-sized horses left the arena with their handlers just as Gelding Other Breeds was announced.

'That's us!' Becky squeaked. 'I mean, that's Charlie and me!'

'Good luck!' Pree and I sang out at once. As the proud owners of mares, we had to wait until the geldings had competed before it was our turn.

Becky led Charlie into the arena. As a part-Arab, he was eligible for Arab and Arab Derivative Led and Ridden Classes at other shows, but in a small show such as this one, Charlie was relegated to Other Breeds.

The bay gelding looked perfect. He was perfect. Becky had owned him since she was seven and they'd been through a lot of good and bad times together. They had a bond, a totally unmistakable bond that even the most unhorsy person in the world could clearly see. He trusted her and she him. They took their place behind an oil-black Friesian, whose long wavy mane and tail were as stunning as his coat was shiny.

The Friesian was taken around the course of cones by his handler, the judge inspected him and then she returned to her position at the fourth cone. Becky looked to me quickly and I gave her the thumbs up. The Friesian was gorgeous and I wouldn't have wanted to compete against him. But I knew that if Becky just believed that she had the most amazing gelding at the show, there was a good chance the judge would agree with her. Flea had made it very clear at Riding Club that Western breed showing is partly about attitude — and boy was he good at showing attitude! Sure, your horse had to look good and respond to your signals. But if you as the handler lacked confidence or looked like you didn't want to be there, you were sending out a clear message to the judge — *I don't want to win this class. Give the blue ribbon to someone else!*

Becky stood on Charlie's nearside, held the lead at the chain with her right hand and gathered the rest of the lead in a loop in her left. She stood straight, tall and proud, just as she should. The judge gave her a nod and she tugged gently on the chain, taking a step forward. Charlie followed. As she approached the judge she tugged on the lead again and he began to jog. She jogged with him around the third cone and to the fourth where she halted him and started setting him up for inspection. A few pushes, pulls and tugs and he was standing like a statue, his ears pricked forward, his eyes alert. Perfect. The judge approached Becky and, remembering the quarter method, she stepped into the judge's opposite half. The judge changed sides and she stepped again. And again and again. Finally the judge moved back to the cone. Becky stayed put with Charlie. Her face was intense. She was concentrating so hard.

Three other geldings were put through their paces then the announcer asked the handlers to turn their backs to the judge to show their numbers. The judge spoke with the announcer for a moment then headed for the line of horses and their waiting handlers.

The pink fifth place ribbon was given to a buckskin, fourth place white went to a chestnut Welsh Cob and third was handed to a girl with a huge grey gelding with the cleanest, whitest, silkiest tail I had ever seen. There were only two ribbons left and two horses — Charlie and the Friesian. Pree and I grabbed each other's hands and waited. I crossed my feet for luck. The judge took a step towards Becky and handed her the red second place ribbon. The blue was handed to the Friesian's handler.

'That was awesome, Beck!' I squealed as she left the arena with Charlie.

Becky wiped her forehead with her hand. 'I'm so glad it's over. I always get so freaked out right before a show, then one event under my belt and I'm right.'

Pree giggled. 'You could fit at least seventy-three events under that belt — the buckle, anyway!'

'Pree — that's us!' My tummy did a flip-flop as I heard the marshalling man at the gate calling for Filly or Mare Other Breeds to enter the arena.

'Get to the back of the line, Spiller, and what was your name again? Pee?' Carly Barnes yanked on

Destiny's lead and the white mare took a small step forward.

'Just watch your big mouth,' I snapped. 'And your horse. Why can't you be decent to her?'

Carly spun on her Western boots. 'Don't you dare tell me what to do with my horse! Don't you ever.'

'Last call for Filly or Mare Other Breeds,' the marshalling man bellowed.

Carly yanked again and Destiny followed her into the arena. She was glowing. But there was something not quite right about her.

'Pree,' I hissed. 'Pree, did you see that?'

Pree scowled. 'Sorry, I'm still recovering from "Pee". What a Creep that kid is!'

'Welcome to my life,' I muttered, giving Honey's lead rope a gentle tug. 'Have a look at Destiny, will you? She's favouring her near foreleg.'

Pree squinted. 'Hard to say.'

'She is, she is. I'm positive.' I glared so hard at Destiny's foot, if I'd had laser-beam eyes, I'd have given her a tattoo.

'You girls entered in this class or not?' the marshal said. His face was red.

I nodded and tugged a little more. 'Yes, sir!'

He laughed and gave me an enormous salute. 'That's more like it!'

The marshal closed the arena gate behind Pree. I gaped with horror. There were only the three of us in this class.

Carly led Destiny to the first cone and waited. She squared the mare up, but Destiny was refusing to put all her weight on her near foreleg.

'Psst,' I hissed at Carly's back. 'Psst.'

She looked up from Destiny's foot and glared. 'Whaddya want?'

'She's sore,' I whispered. 'Pull out.'

Carly tipped back her head and laughed, silently. 'As if!'

'She's limping,' I said, a little louder, a little more urgently. 'I swear, I'm not tricking you.'

Carly waved sweetly at me and turned her back. The judge nodded. She tugged on her lead and they were off.

By the time they went into the jog Destiny was clearly limping. Carly pulled her up at the last cone and tried to square her up again and place all four of her feet in the perfect position. But the mare was tender. She barely touched the sand floor of the arena with the tip of her hoof. The judge inspected her and spoke intensely with Carly for a few moments. Carly said something and shook her head. The judge lifted Destiny's foot and set it down gently, then they spoke again. I was almost wriggling with curiosity. What were they saying? The judge must have noticed, but what was Carly telling her? I had to find out.

The judge returned to her cone and I moved Honey into position at the first cone. I squared her up, pushing, pulling and tugging until I was satisfied that her feet were placed as squarely as possible. Just when I was happy she shifted the weight on her offside hind leg and her back feet went out of place. I sneaked a look at Carly who, rather than being concerned for her horse, was pointing at Honey's feet and laughing.

I faced the judge and focussed my eyes on hers, making sure my shoulders lined up with hers. I had to walk, then jog at the judge. I knew she'd step back out of the way, and that her position was the best for her to observe Honey, but jogging a horse at a human being was something I was definitely not used to.

I held the chain near Honey's cheek with my right hand and held the loops of the leather lead with my left, took a deep breath, stood up straight and fixed what I hoped was the most confident look I could muster on my face.

The judge nodded. I clucked my tongue and tugged the chain and Honey walked beside me. As we neared the second cone, where the judge was standing, I clucked my tongue again, tugged again and broke into a jog. Honey followed suit. I jogged her past the second cone, around the third in a wide semicircle and to the fourth, then in a straight line to the fifth where I pulled her up. We had basically travelled in a sideways U-shape.

I set about squaring her up again, pushing and pulling on the chain, even pushing her chest and tapping her hooves with my feet. She did it again, resting her back foot just as I was happy with her position.

'Whoa,' I murmured. 'Stand up. Stand still.'

I loosened the lead and grabbed her tailbone and gave it a bit of a yank. She stood up properly on her back legs. I was happy with that.

I returned to her head and gave her nose a quick pat. She was trying and I had to reward her for that.

The judge approached us. I watched her carefully. The second she stepped across Honey's tail I moved to the other side in a three-step motion. She walked around Honey, examining her legs and the way she was standing. Honey seemed to know she was on show. She lifted her head nicely and pricked her ears forward, watching the judge as she passed her nose. I three-stepped to the other side, making sure the judge was in the safe quarter the entire time. I stood straight and proud on the outside, although my guts were twisting like mad on the inside.

The judge approached Honey's head for a second time. 'May I see her teeth?'

I gulped, but tried to remain focussed. I hadn't seen this coming. I'd never been asked to show Honey's teeth by any judge at any event. I slid my thumb into the corner of her mouth and wriggled until she lifted her top lip. The judge had a look inside and smiled.

'Thank you.'

She walked away and I three-stepped back, ensuring my back was never turned to her for a minute.

It was Pree's turn. Jasmine has the sweetest nature in the world, apart from Cassata, but she's not the most athletic horse. I crossed my fingers and toes and tried to remain in my perfect handler statue position while watching my friend in her first Halter Class.

Pree clucked and tugged and encouraged and begged, but Jazz didn't raise more than a calm, steady walk, watching her mistress jogging beside her with sweet curiosity.

Pree finally made it to the last cone where she pulled up Jasmine and set her up for inspection. I couldn't see her, but from the grunting noises coming from her direction I could tell that Jazz was a little less than willing to stand in the perfect Halter Class position.

'That'll do,' I heard Pree sigh. The judge inspected Jazz and thanked Pree, then made a beeline for the announcer. She returned with three ribbons — a yellow, a red and a blue.

I muttered a quick prayer to the horse gods: *I don't care if Pree beats me, that would be awesome. And I'm sure she'd feel the same way about me. But don't let the winner be Carly. Please don't let us be beaten by Carly.*

The judge had the yellow ribbon in her hand. I squeezed my eyes shut, not wanting to see her coming for me or Pree. I waited and waited but nothing happened. I opened one eye and then the other and craned my neck to my left. Pree was yellow ribbon-less. It couldn't be!

I looked to my right and there was Carly, her face redder than her hair, clutching the yellow third place ribbon. She caught me watching her and ran her finger across her throat then pointed savagely at me with the ribbon. I was shocked. Not by her menacing gesture, I was used to those. But by her placing. Jasmine had refused to jog or be moulded into the correct position. But then again, Jazz wasn't limping.

The judge had the red ribbon in her hand. She was coming my way. I didn't care which ribbon was mine. Now that I knew Carly wouldn't be able to gloat, it was like I'd won first prize, anyway. I smiled at the judge, ready to accept the red. After all, I hadn't expected to be asked to show her Honey's teeth and I wasn't completely sure I'd done a good enough job for first place. But she walked right past me and handed the red ribbon to Pree, who was barely able to contain herself. I looked over Honey's shoulder, caught Pree's eye and gave her the thumbs up. We couldn't yell and shriek with joy just yet. That would come in about two minutes.

The judge appeared suddenly in front of me. I puffed out my chest and smiled some more.

'Well done.' She handed me the blue ribbon. A blue first place ribbon!

I accepted it, stoked beyond words. 'Thank you.' It was all I could manage.

The announcer asked that we leave the arena and I three-stepped again to Honey's nearside. The show wasn't over and I wanted to make sure we left looking as switched on as we had when we'd competed.

Carly was the first to leave. Honey and I followed, our first Western ribbon soured by the sight of Destiny limping. I knew the limp had cost them a higher placing.

Once we'd cleared the arena for the Colt or Stallion Other Breeds Class, Carly turned.

'I s'pose you think you're better than me? I s'pose you think your horse is better than mine?'

'According to you, my horse is a mule, so I don't know what you're so worried about,' I quipped. 'But seriously, pull out. Destiny's limping. It's worse than it was five minutes ago.'

'She's not your horse.' Carly pulled at Destiny's lead. 'So mind your own business.'

Carly dragged Destiny away in the direction of the floats. I hung back, waiting for Pree. Becky was there in an instant with Charlie.

'What was that all about?' Becky said.

'Wow, she's a tough cookie, isn't she, Ash? Becky? She reminds me of this one time at preschool when I was in the sandpit and I wanted this bucket and another girl wanted the bucket too and so we both yanked on it and she won and whacked me in the head—'

'She doesn't matter,' I said firmly. 'But Destiny needs our help.'

sixteen

Western Showmanship

'You ready for Showmanship?' Pree tapped my shoulder and chewed on a hot dog she'd bought from the dilapidated bus turned kiosk. It was morning tea time and I was stuffing my face with slices of sweet, crunchy apple. Crunching has always calmed me down when I'm nervous. Pree, on the other hand, was really enjoying her hot dog. Her mouth was so full it looked like two wild animals were wrestling behind her cheeks.

'Hardly,' I said, swallowing another slice of apple.

'You just won a blue ribbon.' Pree opened her mouth as wide as a hippo and took an enormous bite of hot dog. The dog part slipped out of the bread and landed *splat* in the sawdust. 'Oh, no!'

'That's tragic,' I said, staring at the half-eaten and now filthy hot dog. 'Poor Preencess! Want some of my apple?'

Pree shook her head and continued eating the bread roll.

'The blue ribbon was great,' I said, 'but that was a Halter Class. Flea says Halter is a walk in the park compared to Showmanship.'

'You're doing Beginner/Youth. It's basically the same as Halter.'

'Except for the pivot,' I said, my stomach flip-flopping — I'm sure all those slices of apple were tumbling around inside. 'It's the pivot that's freaking me out. And don't forget she's s'posed to jog, not trot, and the jog is different.'

I held tight to Honey's lead and prayed. I didn't care about winning. I didn't care what colour ribbon I got, or if I got one at all. All I cared about was not making a fool of myself. Not too many Creekers had entered Showmanship. There was Flea, of course, and Carly. But apart from them, there was only me. Becky had decided to wait until the next show and focus all her energy on the Hunter Under Saddle classes. She was entering four classes so I could see why she was a little preoccupied. I was starting to feel that waiting for the next show could be the way to go myself, but I'd already paid my entry fee and couldn't back out. There was another thing, far more important than the money. I don't like quitting. It's not what I'm usually about. I had to do the class.

'I don't think I can eat this now. Do you?' Pree tapped at her half-eaten and very grotty frankfurt with the toe of her boot.

I shook my head.

'Well, good luck, Ash. I'll be watching. Just remember to never touch the chain, okay? Never touch the chain!'

'Never touch the chain,' I chanted. 'Never touch the chain.'

'Stop me if you've heard this one.'

'I hate to tell you, Preezy-Boo, but I've heard you say that at least a thousand times.' I smiled at my friend.

Pree wrinkled her nose. 'Huh? Anyway, what do you call a horse that likes arts and crafts? A hobby horse! D'you get it? A hobby horse!'

Pree gave me a quick hug and a wave and headed back to the kiosk. I led Honey to the arena to wait for our class to be called.

★ ★ ★

I couldn't believe it was happening. My first Showmanship Class was underway. There were more entrants than I'd expected. Flea was showing the same gorgeous gelding. I felt instantly that I had no chance against him. There was something totally different about him in his gear and hat, and it wasn't just that he looked different. It was his whole presence. He was like a different person.

Carly, on the other hand, was her usual noxious self, baring her teeth and growling at me as I entered the arena. Apart from Queen Creep and Flea and me, there were another seven horses and handlers entered.

'What are you doing in this class?' I hissed as I led Honey past Destiny. 'Your horse is lame.'

'Fat lot you know, Spiller.' Carly spat out my hated nickname like it was bitter. 'She's fine, as you can see.'

I looked at Destiny's legs. 'I can see she's bandaged now.'

Carly's face went pale. 'Nothing in the rules to say her legs can't be bandaged. They're exercise bandages. That's all.'

I said nothing but raised my eyebrows. I didn't trust her. This was, after all, the same girl who'd been sponsored to go to the Waratah Grove Junior Cross-Country Riding Championships by the entire town and had let everyone down by being disqualified. The reason for her disqualification? Dangerous riding.

'I'm watching you, Carly Barnes,' I said.

Carly laughed. 'Ooh, I'm *sooo* scared.'

She turned away and focussed on the judge.

I tried to forget about Destiny. She wasn't my horse and so, technically, wasn't my problem, or so my head was quietly saying. But my heart was screaming. Destiny was lame, I was convinced of that.

The Western music washed over Honey and me. For a Western rookie, Honey was doing well. She had been perfect all day and had been trying over and over again to please me. Now, if I could just do justice to her faith in me by turning in a good performance, I'd be happy.

Three handlers had their turns and I took the chance to really get to know the course. Four cones had been set up in an L-shape. We were to start at the first, then walk to the second where we were to pivot to the right. Then we were supposed to jog to and around the third to the right again and stop at the fourth for inspection. It was easy, apart from that pivot, and getting Honey to jog. And having her respond to my commands without laying so much as a fingertip on the chain. And getting her set up nice and square. And doing the quarter method without ending up tangled in my lead or Honey's legs!

Flea took his turn around the course. If I hadn't been so embarrassed to live next door to him I would have felt proud. For a boy nicknamed after a nasty parasite, he was an amazing Western handler. He'd win the class for sure. And if he didn't, I'd eat my boots. Carly followed Flea onto the course. Destiny seemed to walk okay until the pivot. Maybe it was the pressure on her leg or the way she was being asked to use it, but she stumbled and, when she righted herself, she refused to stand on the foreleg. If Carly couldn't see her lameness there was something wrong with her. Well, more wrong than usual.

Finally it was my turn. I stood with Honey at the first cone, the one that simply marked out the starting point of the course. I waited and watched for the judge's nod.

On the nod I tugged on Honey's lead, strictly on the leather, and took a step. Honey followed, which made me sigh with relief. Temporary relief. We neared the next cone. It was here that we had to pivot. I knew it was a long shot, but I hoped we'd manage it okay. At the cone I took a step to the right, then twisted my body in a tight circle. The idea was that Honey would spin on her offside foreleg and come back to a perfectly straight position. That wasn't quite the way it worked out. She swung her rump around okay, but took at least five huge steps with her forelegs to do it rather than keep one foreleg on the ground and delicately cross the other to get herself around.

I pushed the mistake to the back of my mind. It was time to jog and the distance between the cones seemed as long as a marathon. I tugged again and broke into a jog. It took a little while to convince Honey, but eventually she followed me. I wasn't sure that her gait was strictly a jog, but it was the best I could do.

We jogged to and around the third cone then on again to the fourth. I stopped and Honey stopped beside me. I took a few seconds to set her up nice and square, then waited for the judge. The judge approached and I immediately began my three-step from side to side, always keeping her in the safe quarter. She cleared us to move off and we lined up beside Carly.

Another four handlers followed and then the places were announced. I was very happy with my pink fifth place ribbon and I wasn't surprised to see Flea with the blue ribbon in his hand. Carly looked like she wanted to rip her brown eighth place ribbon to shreds. Once the class was dismissed, Carly was approached by the judge again. I strained my ears to hear what they were saying but all I could hear were guitars twanging. Carly didn't seem too pleased with what was being said to her. She went all red in the face and made a rather rude gesture at the judge as she walked away. She yanked Destiny from the arena and the white mare tripped away like she was walking barefoot across a bindi patch on a scorching summer's day.

I couldn't just sit back and do nothing knowing Destiny was hurt. Somehow I had to help her.

'You with me?' I hissed. My friends and I were tiptoeing along the row of stables at Pinebark Ridge Western Riding Club. We were on a mission.

'Absolutely,' Pree said, nodding.

'You bet.' Becky wanted in as well.

It was lunch break, and handlers were transforming themselves into riders, swapping their spangles for crisp white shirts, their jeans for joddies and their cowboy hats for helmets. Becky, Pree and I had changed, too. I hadn't planned on riding in Western Pleasure — I'd realized early on at Riding Club that Honey wouldn't be ready for that for a long time! But barrel racing was coming up and there was no way I would be going home without having a go at my favourite event.

Our horses were resting in the shade and snacking on a haynet each under the close supervision of Julie and Jodie Ferguson. Once I'd told them of my plan they'd been only too happy to help.

Carly had booked stabling for the show. I'd never known her to do that before. She usually just hung around her float or the Shady Creek Riding Club camp. Or around Becky and me, bugging us and making us both think seriously of careers in pest control.

'First we find her stable, then we find out what she's got in there.'

'What do you mean?' Pree wrinkled her nose.

'She's up to something,' I said. 'It's those bandages. I just know she's done something to Destiny.'

I spotted a white head at the end of the aisle and stopped dead. Pree slammed into me from behind.

'What's going on?'

'Shh. I see her!'

The mare was standing still in her stall. I could hear thumping and scraping. I grabbed my friends by their arms and yanked them into the nearest empty stall just as Carly's head appeared.

We pressed our backs hard against the wall of the stall, praying that she wouldn't hear our breathing and waited for the sound of her footsteps to become more and more faint.

'Has she gone?' Pree whispered.

Becky shrugged. 'Can't tell.'

'Let's go,' I said. 'What's the worst thing that can happen?'

'The McManiacs will be waiting to pounce on us then go crying to Mrs Mac,' Pree said, a huge grin on her face.

I shook my head. 'Forget about Savannah and Mikenzie. Think!'

'Um, Carly'll be in the stall?' Pree shrugged.

'And what's the best thing that can happen?' I poked Becky in the ribs.

'Carly won't be in the stall and we'll get to the bottom of this business with Destiny's foot.' Becky grinned.

'Right,' I said. 'So let's go.'

We crept out of the stall and down the aisle until we reached Destiny. The mare was standing very still, and to our great relief, she was alone.

'Check that out,' I said, pointing. An ice pack was strapped to her leg.

'What's this?' Pree held up a tube. 'It was on the floor.'

Becky took a close look. 'It's bute.'

'It's what?' I grabbed the tube from Pree and read the label. 'Phenyl ... what on earth is this stuff?'

Becky clucked her tongue. 'It's Phenylbutazone.'

'Come again?' Pree stared at Becky with wide eyes.

'Bute's just a nickname,' Becky explained. 'It's an anti-inflammatory cream. You rub it on a horse's leg to reduce pain and swelling.'

'You think Carly's been using it today?' I said. 'Look, she's just left Destiny's bandages in a pile on the floor. That's so dangerous. Typical of—'

'What're you doing?' Pree said as Becky opened Destiny's stall.

'I'm gonna check out those bandages. I know what bute smells like. I bet Destiny's been smeared in the stuff and Carly's tried to cover it up.'

I looked over my shoulder. We could talk our way out of being in the stables, but explaining what Becky was doing inside Destiny's stall would be sticky.

Becky snatched up the bandages and slipped out of the stall in a heartbeat. She held the bandages to her face. 'It's bute all right.'

I was shocked. 'That's disgusting. Who would try to cover up their horse's injury just to go in a show?'

'We have to examine Destiny's foot,' Becky said. 'It must be serious.'

'We're not vets, Becky,' Pree said. 'Besides, she's got an ice pack on. What if we make it worse?'

'We're just going to look.' Becky squeezed Pree's hand. 'We'll put it straight back on.'

'Pree, you stand guard,' I said. 'Becky, just roll the ice pack up a little.'

Becky squeezed back into the stall. I followed suit.

Pree was bouncing from one foot to another. 'We'll get caught!'

'We have less chance of getting caught if you stand guard by the stable door,' Becky said. 'Go!'

Pree jogged away. I rubbed Destiny's chest and looked into her eyes. She was quiet and seemed to have lost her sparkle. I could tell she was in pain. Her head was low and she was ignoring her haynet.

Becky loosened and rolled up the ice pack. I knelt beside Destiny and laid my hand on her fetlock. It was hot, despite the ice pack. And swollen, too.

'There's something wrong,' I said. 'I have to look at her foot.'

'Quick,' Becky hissed. 'We're running out of time.'

'She's coming!' Pree cried. 'I can see her.'

My heart thumped. I could just bail. I could run away with Becky and Pree and have no chance of being caught interfering with another rider's horse, which could see us all eliminated. But that would mean leaving Destiny to suffer, and that was something I just couldn't do.

'Quick,' Becky said again.

I ran my hand down Destiny's leg and clucked my tongue. 'Up.'

The white mare lifted her foot. I pressed down gently on her sole, taking care around her frog. I looked hard. It was shaded in the stall and hard to see, but there was a mark, like a small hole, near the wall of her toe. I touched it gingerly. It felt odd.

Hot, again, with a soft bump the size of a five cent piece.

I set her foot down and Becky rolled the ice pack back into place. I patted Destiny's chest again and we slipped out of the stall, one after the other.

'Pree!' I hissed. 'Come on.'

Pree spun on the spot and dashed back to the stall where Becky and I were waiting. 'She's so close. We've gotta get out of here.'

We linked arms and ran down the aisle past a Palouse Pony and the stunning Friesian gelding who'd beaten Charlie in the Halter Class.

'What're you lot doing here?' came a voice from behind us.

Becky, Pree and I skidded to a halt.

'Nothing,' I said. 'Just came for a closer look at the little bloke.' I indicated the Palouse Pony.

Carly scowled. 'Get outta here. You're not allowed in without a stable booking.'

Becky saluted. 'No worries.'

We left the stable block in silence, relieved to have completed our mission without being caught, but consumed with worry over Destiny. We knew something was wrong, we knew Carly had tried to cover it up, but we couldn't prove either without incriminating ourselves. We could only hope that Carly would come to her senses and withdraw from the rest of the show before it was too late.

I was on my way to check on the horses when I slammed into a tall and very pretty blonde girl.

'Sorry,' I mumbled. 'I wasn't looking where—'

'Ash! *Come stai?* How are ya?' The blonde gazed down at me through thick layers of make-up. Her hair was cropped to her ears, like a boy's, but she didn't look boyish. She had sparkly earrings and a pendant around her neck made from coloured glass. There was something familiar about her, but completely unfamiliar at the same time. She smiled at me. I recognised the braces with the hot pink elastics immediately.

'Jenna? Is that you?'

seventeen

Sitting Pretty

It couldn't be her, could it? I stood frozen to the spot, too confused to move.

The blonde wrapped her arms around my neck and smooshed me into her chest. I drew back and stared at her tiny T-shirt that showed more than it hid. At her short shorts and endless tanned legs. At the huge furry boots on her feet and the gum that rolled around in her mouth. At the bangles on her arms and the boy's name drawn on her hand in blue pen. 'What happened to you?'

Jenna threw back her head and tinkled. 'I grew up. You should try it some time.'

'You're here,' I said feebly, still a little shocked that

the almost unrecognisable girl standing before me was Jenna.

'I came a week early, to surprise you. Your mum snuck out and picked me up. *Sei sorpresa?* Are you surprised?'

'In more ways than one.' I took a step back. 'How was Italy?'

Jenna sighed and her face went all dreamy. '*Italia! Si, si. La bella Italia.*'

'How's your mum?'

Jenna rolled her eyes. 'She's been much better since she started seeing her boyfriend.'

'Your mum has a boyfriend?' I couldn't believe it. I knew Jenna's parents were separated, but I couldn't imagine them being with other people. It was just too weird.

'*Si chiama Antonio.* His name's Antonio. She met him in Rome.' Jenna chewed hard on her wad of bright pink gum and looked around. 'What is this place? I've gotta tell you, Ash. It's a real shock being back in Shady Creek. *Italia* is so beautiful at this time of year.'

'It's a riding club. They do Western here. It's my first time.' I knew I was babbling. For some reason I felt nervous. I needed a carrot. Now.

'Wow, horses really stink, don't they? *Puzza!*' Jenna wrinkled her nose and fluffed out her hair with her fingers.

'They don't stink!' I said.

Jenna smiled at me like I needed to have something very easy explained to me step by step. 'Of course *you* don't think they smell. You're around them so much you've gotten used to it. When I think of it, you've always smelled a bit like horses.'

I stared at her with my mouth hanging open. Who was this creature and what had she done with my best friend?

Jenna dug in her tiny backpack and pulled out some lipgloss and a compact mirror. After checking her face in the mirror, she carefully reapplied the gloss. 'I saw a cowboy before.'

I nodded. 'It's a Western Show. The place is crawling with them.'

'Ooh, crawling with cowboys!' Jenna smacked her freshly glossed lips together. 'Let's go and check some out.'

She turned on her furry boots and jogged daintily towards the arena wall. I stared after her, frozen. She stopped after a few steps and turned to me, beckoning frantically. I took a step towards her and she smiled so wide her braces reflected the sunlight. Right at that moment Carly rode past on Destiny. The mare was walking slowly, taking step after careful step. Her forelegs were wrapped again and, unless you were looking for it, you never would have noticed a limp. Carly was out of her Western gear and now wearing her cream joddies, white shirt and black Hunter jacket. Her black helmet sat neatly on her head.

'Pull out, Carly!' I called.

Carly looked down at me. Her face was so pale that her freckles looked dark and angry.

'Mind your own business, Spiller.'

'I am minding my own business. And Destiny's, too. She can't speak so I'm speaking for her. She's a beautiful mare and you're gonna ruin her, all for a stupid ribbon.'

Carly went red. 'I don't have to listen to you. You're a nobody. You're a nothing. So why don't you pack up your ugly mule and go back to the city where you belong.'

She kicked Destiny hard behind her girth and the mare walked away. I stared after them, shaking my head. Some people just don't deserve horses.

'Ashleigh, *avanti!* Would you come on!' Jenna was perched on the arena wall.

I waved to her. Now that Jenna was here I was certain things would be just like they were before. Sure, she looked a little different, but deep down inside I knew she was the same old Jenna. A haircut and a pair of furry boots couldn't really change somebody. Could they?

'How's Jenna settling in?' Mum tousled my hair as I poured myself my before-bed glass of milk.

'Fine,' I said. 'So far she's settled into her old three drawers, plus two of mine and half of my wardrobe. She's also settled into two shelves in my bathroom and the entire shower caddy. I never knew one person could need so many bottles and tubes.'

'Was it a nice surprise?' Mum looked hopeful. 'Your dad and I thought you'd be, what's that word you use? Oh yeah, stoked!'

'Yeah. I was really stoked.' I tried to smile, but my face felt all tight. Let's face it. When you're not smiling on the inside it's awfully hard to smile on the outside.

'Where is she?'

'Still in the shower,' I said, shrugging.

Mum stared up at the ceiling. 'Still? Wow.'

'I don't know what she's doing in there but she's locked the door and—'

Mum smiled. 'Her mum did say we mightn't recognise her.'

I helped myself to a chocolate chip biscuit from the jar. I didn't usually eat right before bed, but I was stressed and I always eat when I'm stressed. 'Well, I wish someone had told *me* how different she is. Why am I always the last to know all the important stuff?'

'Such as?' Mum folded her arms.

I put down my milk and my biscuit and folded my arms right back. 'Such as us moving to the country and you having Jason and Dad quitting his job—'

'He didn't quit.' Mum held up her hand, stop-sign style.

'He may as well have,' I said. I took a bite of my biscuit and chewed, but instantly felt sick and thrust it at Mum. I drank deeply from my glass. Ah, better.

I put my glass in the sink, kissed Mum goodnight and went back to my room. Jenna was sitting on the floor. She was wearing a pink silky singlet and matching boxer shorts, and had a towel wrapped around her head. I looked down at my favourite old nightie with the iron-on transfer of an Arab. It was peeling off at the edges and very faded, but it was like a second skin. I had always loved it. It seemed so babyish though, in the presence of Jenna's glamorous pyjamas. I folded my arms, hoping she wouldn't notice.

'What're you doing?' I said. It was bedtime and I was tired. After a full show day I was ready to hit the hay. Literally.

'Pedicure,' she said. 'Mum got me this cool pedicure set in *Firenze*, Florence. Every Sunday night I give myself a complete pedicure and paint my toenails. It's so important to always look your best.'

'Do you wanna use the computer?' I said, sitting on the edge of my bed.

'I don't use the computer much any more. Only for chatting. Oh, and emailing *miei amici*, my friends, in Italy.' Jenna blew on her toes.

I felt hollow, empty, like there was a hole in my heart — like something precious inside had sneaked away before I could do anything to stop it. If Jenna wasn't Jenna Dawson, computer freak, I didn't know who she was any more. At least I knew now why her emails had run dry. To me, anyway.

'Want some?' Jenna offered me her bottle of nail polish.

I shook my head. 'No thanks.'

Jenna cocked her head to the side and scrutinized me. 'You know, Ash. You'd be really pretty if you'd fix your hair and put on a bit of make-up. I know!' Jenna's eyes widened and she clapped her hands. 'I'll give you a makeover. Teach you to put on make-up and do your hair. Maybe get some nice clothes. Whaddya say?'

I shrugged. 'Dunno, Jen. It's not really—'

'Oh, go on. Let me! It'll be the coolest fun.' Jenna packed up her army of bottles, tubes and scissors.

'I don't think Mum and Dad would like—'

Jenna laughed. '*Non m'importa!* Who cares what *they* say?'

'I do,' I said. My voice was small.

Jenna gave me a look, the same one she'd given me at the show. Like I didn't understand the simplest, easiest, most basic things in the universe. 'You're turning twelve soon. You need to grow up, Ash. And I'm gonna be the one to show you how to do it. *Ascoltami* — listen to me and do what I say and in two weeks you'll be as *matura*, mature, as me.'

Jenna reached both her hands under her singlet between her shoulder blades and fidgeted. In a second or two she pulled out something long and elasticy.

'Is that a . . .' I almost choked on the word. 'Bra?'

Jenna rolled her eyes. '*Certo!* Of course! Are you wearing one yet?'

I shook my head. 'No. Should I be?'

'I'm twelve. You're nearly twelve. Personally I wouldn't be caught dead without one.'

I tossed back my covers, crawled into bed and stared at the wall. 'Turn out the light when you're done.'

'You got it,' Jenna said. '*Buona notte!* Good night!' She rustled, scraped, brushed and towelled for a few minutes, then switched off the light and climbed into bed. The same bed she'd slept in just nine months earlier when she'd stayed for the summer holidays.

I lay awake long after Jenna's deep rhythmic breathing told me she was fast asleep. Then I turned over in bed and watched her. In her sleep she looked like the same old Jenna. My chest ached and ached. I missed her. She was right here, in my room. But I missed her. I wondered if she'd ever go back to normal or if the new Jenna was here to stay.

Finally I fell into a fitful sleep and dreamed of armies of giant bottles of nail polish chasing me, chanting, 'Makeover! Makeover!' I woke up, sweating and breathing hard. It was twenty-eight minutes past one in the morning. Jenna slept soundly. But my pulse was racing. I was afraid. What did all this grown-up stuff mean? Could Jenna and I still be friends? Would she still like me, even though I wasn't *matura* like her? The only thing scarier than the questions that whirled through my head were the answers that followed hot on their heels.

eighteen

Maturity Bites

'What happened to Jenna?' Becky Cho grabbed my arm and tugged until my ear was close to her face. We stood together in my corral and stared at Jenna, who was lying by the pool in a bikini, reading a magazine she'd brought with her. She hadn't been interested in joining us at all. She hadn't been interested in much all week. I shook my head in disgust that anyone could bear to bare so much in this weather. Jenna's goose bumps were so enormous that each one practically needed its own zip code.

I shrugged my shoulders and rubbed Honey's forelock. 'I wish I knew. But at the moment I can only think of one person in the entire world who's more obnoxious.'

'Rachael.' Becky looked into my eyes. 'There's no contest.'

'Uh-uh. Savannah McMurray.'

Becky shuddered. 'Don't mention her name. Did I tell you about how she kept staring at me at the show? And how she laughed her head off when you didn't get a place in barrel racing?'

I grimaced. 'Yes, you did tell me, and if you don't mind, I'm trying to put it behind me. You know, there are some times when I'm totally happy that I don't work at Shady Trails any more.'

'You sure?'

I smiled and shook my head. 'No.'

Becky smiled and squeezed my hand. 'Mrs McMurray'll take you back. You just wait.'

I didn't want to talk about it. I couldn't talk about it. I had to change the subject.

'Anyone interested in going shopping?' came a voice from behind the fence.

Jenna was wrapped in a large pink beach towel. She was shivering.

'You wanna go riding?' I called, hopeful.

Jenna snorted. 'Are you serious? I'll get my fingernails dirty. I touched that horse yesterday and actually broke a nail. And every time I set foot near a horse I have to soak in the bath for an hour to get the smell out of my skin. Do you think I'm *pazza*, nuts?'

Becky stared at Jenna, her mouth hanging open. I stepped forward.

'You go right ahead, Jen. We immature kids are happy out here in the dirt playing with our smelly horses.'

Jenna made a 'W' with her hands. 'Whatever. *Ciao*.'

She walked into the house through the kitchen door, slamming it hard behind her.

'What was that?'

'Good question.' I rolled my eyes and ran the dandy-brush over Honey's back. Her skin rippled.

'I can't believe her,' Becky said. 'She's like some alien.'

'From planet Brat,' I said.

I finished grooming Honey and lowered her saddle onto her back. Honey tossed her head as I did up her girth.

'Looking forward to a ride, girl?' I said, smiling. I felt guilty about going without Jenna, but she'd made up her mind — shopping beat horses, hooves down.

The kitchen door slammed again and I peered over Honey's back. Jenna was dressed in tight blue jeans, sandals and an expensive-looking jacket. She'd done her hair and painted her lips with more of that pink gloss.

'*Piu tardi, ragazzi!* Later, girls!' she called, blowing Becky and me a kiss. Then she walked down the driveway on her tippy-toes and pulled a cell phone from her teeny backpack.

'How was shopping?' I smiled as wide as I could manage at Jenna when she came home that night. My best friend had been gone all day and I had been worried out of my mind and feeling sick with guilt.

'*Terribile!* Awful. I don't know how you can stand it here, Ash!' Jenna cried, throwing half a dozen plastic shopping bags on the bedroom floor. 'It's like the bush. There are no shops, no boys, and the weather is murder on your skin. I can't wait to get back to the city.'

'Are you hungry?' I pushed the words I really wanted to say down to the very pit of my guts. Mum had gone to a lot of trouble to make home-made lasagne with caesar salad, one of her yummiest dinners, and I was starving. We'd put off serving until Jenna came home and now that she was finally here it was time to eat.

'I had a burger, hope you don't mind.' Jenna pulled her lipgloss out of her backpack and smeared it on, then checked herself in the mirror. 'And I made a friend today. I've invited her round. She'll be here in ten.'

'What? Who?'

'The coolest chick. She's from *Inghilterra*, England. Finally someone around here who speaks my language.'

'England?' I said, trying to stay calm. 'Did you say England?'

The doorbell rang. I had this terrible feeling all of a sudden. I wanted to crawl inside the nearest hollow log and not come out until I was convinced that Shady Creek was completely mature-girls free.

Jenna ran downstairs for the door. I heard it swing open and the high-pitched chatter and giggling of two new friends.

'Ash! *Vieni qui*. Come here.' Jenna's voice danced up the stairs.

I took one step after another, my toes heavy with dread. Right there in my doorway was the one person I had hoped to never see again, let alone have to welcome into my home.

'Hello, Savannah,' I said.

'Ashleigh Miller! Your house is so small. Ha! My house back home is ten times this size. Ha!'

Savannah flicked her long blonde hair around and stepped through the door. She had a small suitcase in one hand, a Jenna-style teeny backpack over her shoulder and a hot pink mobile phone in her free hand.

'Cool phone! *Fantastico*,' Jenna said. 'It's the latest, isn't it?'

The two of them 'oohed' and 'aahed' over it as they made their way past me up the stairs.

'Where are you going?' I called after them. I felt all out of place, like I didn't belong in their neat little circle even though I was standing in my own home.

'Your room,' Jenna said. 'Where else?'

I jogged up after them. 'But why?'

'We wanna hang out there.' Jenna gave me one of those 'Ashleigh doesn't have a clue' looks and exchanged glances with Savannah. They stifled giggles.

I could feel a hot sticky lump rising in my throat. 'I'm gonna have some dinner.'

'Take your time,' Savannah said.

They charged down the hallway and into my room, closing the door behind them. There was a burst of giggling, followed by loud thumping music.

I turned and ran down the stairs, stung. I felt like I'd been bitten all over my body, the biggest, nastiest bite of all right smack in my chest.

Mum, Dad and Jason were sitting at the table.

'Ready to eat, possum?' Mum said. 'Where's Jenna?'

I could feel it coming. I wasn't tough like Carly or brave like Becky or full of jokes and giggles like Pree. I was Ashleigh, plain old immature Ashleigh. I stood in front of my family and burst into tears.

nineteen

All Grown-up

'Ashleigh Miller, you look totally ridiculous,' I said, staring at my reflection in the mirror the next day.

Jenna and Savannah had made me over. I hadn't needed or wanted a makeover, but I'd figured that if I was going to have any chance at all of keeping Jenna I'd better go along with her plan. I didn't care what Savannah thought. She'd ruined Shady Trails for me, but at least I knew that once she went home she'd be unlikely to bother me again for years. Jenna, on the other hand, had been my best friend since preschool. I couldn't lose her. I'd nearly lost her before, when I'd moved to the country. She'd felt like I'd abandoned her and in a way I had, I guess. Then we'd made up and spent the summer together before she went to Italy with her mum and brothers. I'd missed her so much. I'd decided overnight that I'd do anything for our friendship.

But now I had purple stuff smeared on my eyelids, bright red lips, a hairdo that made me look like I'd had a terrible fright, and fingernails painted pink. Jenna had ordered me into a top that buttoned up at the back and showed my belly button, and clipped big silver earrings to my ears. Then she'd squeezed me into tight black jeans with rips at the knees and those big furry boots she'd worn at the Western Show. I felt like a freak. I looked worse. But Jenna and Savannah had squealed with delight and congratulated each other on their success.

Jenna was demonstrating how to put on a padded bra when the doorbell rang.

'I'll get it,' I said, doing my best Frankenstein walk, happy for any excuse to get away from them.

'Becky!' I said, when I opened the door.

Becky stared at me. 'What in leaping Lipizzaners happened to you?'

I rolled my eyes. 'It's a long story.'

Becky covered my mouth with her hand. 'It can wait. Something's happened.'

'Muggorm?'

Becky peeled her hand away from my mouth. 'It's Destiny.'

My heart stopped beating for a moment. 'What's wrong? What happened?'

'Carly called me. She actually called me. She's freaking out.' Becky was almost hysterical.

'Why didn't she call Flea?'

'She said he's hopeless. Besides, he's off at some show today. You know he was High Point Youth at the show on—'

'Doesn't she have any other friends?'

'No. The Creeps don't work that way. Kids don't like them. They're scared of them.'

'What about her parents?'

'Her mum's on a hair job and her dad's at work. She's often at home by herself.'

'Really?' I'd had no idea. It occurred to me then that I didn't know much about Carly Barnes at all. I'd never bothered to find out, either.

'But why do you want to help her?' I couldn't figure it out. Carly had been nothing but venomous to Becky, and to me since my first day in Shady Creek.

'This isn't about Carly, Ash. It's about a horse.'

I nodded. That was so true. Our issues with Carly

and the Creeps would have to wait. This was about Destiny.

'She said to get to her place right away. But I didn't want to go alone.'

'Give me two minutes,' I said.

'I'll saddle Honey for you.' She dashed down the porch stairs and across the lawn. Becky was a true friend.

I hobbled inside, unzipping the jeans. By the time I found Jenna and Savannah they'd switched on the telly and were copying some singer doing a hip-shaking dance.

'Get me out of this top,' I said. 'I have to go.'

Jenna gave me a look. 'Go where?'

'You wouldn't understand.' I kicked off the furry boots.

'I might,' Jenna said, smiling. 'You gotta hot date? That cute guy, that *simpatico*, from next door? He's hot!'

I sighed. 'Of course not. Becky's here and we need to go.'

'Another one that needs our help,' Savannah said, a smug smile playing at her lips.

'I'm not undoing the top until you tell me what's going on.' Jenna stood with her hands on her hips.

The singer on the screen behind her shimmied away, unperturbed.

'It's Destiny, Carly's horse and—'

'*Sei incredibile!* You're unbelievable,' Jenna cried. 'You'll do anything for a dumb horse but you can't spend one day with me doing what I want to do.'

'But it's serious,' I said, shocked. 'Carly's called us for help. She'd never do that unless it was an emergency.'

Jenna shook her head. 'When are you gonna grow up, Ashleigh? Just get over this horse thing. Everyone else does. And by the way, having your twelfth birthday party in the pony party room is just plain immature.'

It hit me then. Right then. Linley Heights *was* the place for me to be. I could be with other people who loved horses. Who lived for and with horses and who would understand that a horse in trouble was so much more important than painted pink fingernails. In fact, it was everything.

'I don't know you any more,' I said. I pulled the top over my head and threw it at her feet. 'If I'm immature for loving horses that's fine with me, Jen. Coz I'd rather be immature and horse mad than all grown-up and heartless like you.'

Jenna's face cracked and for the first time since she had arrived I saw a flash of the old Jenna in her eyes. But I didn't have time to wait. Destiny needed us.

I'd never been to Carly's place before. I'd never wanted to. But now Becky and I pulled up outside a pink house with a sign advertising *Hair by Michelle* hammered into the front lawn.

'This is it,' Becky said, sliding to the ground. She began leading Charlie down the side of the house. 'You ready?'

'Shouldn't we knock? We can't just—'

'She knows we're coming. Besides, there's no time to knock.'

I dismounted, taking Honey's reins under her chin and leading her into Carly's corral.

'You take care of these two,' Becky said. 'I'll head down to the stable. You see it. Just there.' Becky pointed across the yard.

'Whatever you say. But will you be okay? Just you and Carly?'

'I've known her all my life,' Becky said. She was calm. More grown-up than Jenna. So much more sophisticated than Savannah. 'It'll be okay.'

She left me with our horses and ran to the stable and out of sight. I untacked them both, rubbing them down with one of Jason's old cloth nappies. There was a bit of grass to pick at so, after making sure they had clean water to drink, I ran after Becky.

Nothing prepared me for what I saw and I know I'll never forget it. Not the sight nor the smell. Aside from Honey when I first found her, I'd never seen a horse so sick.

Destiny, the gorgeous white mare with a heart as gentle as she was beautiful, was lying on the stable floor soaked in sweat. Her whole body was shaking. She was breathing so fast, like she couldn't suck in enough air. Her tail was stained with diarrhoea. Her foot, the lame foot, was swollen to three times its normal size at her coronet — the part of her hoof that connects to her pastern — and something thick and creamy coloured was seeping from the wall of her hoof. The smell was terrible, like rotten eggs, or really stinky feet. I gagged, covering my nose with my hands. Destiny's eyes had rolled back so that only the whites showed. I couldn't tell whether or not she was conscious.

'What happened?' I was stunned.

Carly looked up. She was kneeling beside her horse, stroking her neck again and again. 'It was after the show. She started to go down. I thought I could handle it.'

'I told you she was lame!' I yelled. 'What's wrong with—'

'Not now, Ash!' Becky was firm. 'There's no time for pointing the finger. We have to get help.'

'What should I do?' Carly cried. 'I don't want her to die!'

My heart softened at once. I knew exactly what it was like to be holding the horse you love in your arms, praying for her to live. Ready to give anything to make her well.

'I'll call Amanda,' Becky said. 'Ash, you stay here with Carly and see if you can get the full story. Amanda will need to know every detail once she gets here.'

Carly didn't say much while Becky was gone. She just kept mumbling something about a nail on the morning of the show.

'Why would you leave it so long?' I said.

Carly looked at me with tired, frightened eyes. 'You're not the only one on a budget.'

I took her hand in mine and held it. We sat side by side, saying nothing, our hands entwined. We stayed like that until Becky came back and then Carly wrenched her hand away.

'When's she coming?' I said.

'She's on her way. She's had to delay some surgery, but she said she'd be here in twenty minutes.' Becky kneeled beside Destiny. 'I called Dad as well.'

Twenty minutes. I only hoped Destiny could wait that long.

Amanda Filano, Shady Creek's brilliant young vet, shook her head. 'Never delay calling me, Carly. The horse's wellbeing always comes first.'

Tears spilled down Carly's cheeks. I'd never seen her cry for real.

'It's hard to be a hundred per cent certain, but I'd say she's got septicaemia. She stepped on a nail, you said?'

Carly nodded, miserable. 'Went right into her foot, up through her sole. I pulled it out. Then we went to the show.'

'You showed her with an injury like that?' Amanda was furious.

Carly nodded. 'I didn't wanna miss out on—'

'There'll always be another show.' Amanda shook her head and ran her hand down Destiny's leg. 'She's had a huge abscess. You can see where the infection has just burst through her foot, like a volcano. Thank goodness it found a way out. This could have been so easily treated. Either me or a farrier could have located and drained an abscess.'

'I'm sorry,' Carly sobbed. 'Will she be okay? Is her hoof ruined?'

'The hoof usually does recover. But it's the infection that worries me. Depending on the bacteria in her bloodstream, she could develop pneumonia or further abscesses in her kidneys, lungs or even her brain. She'll need intravenous antibiotics and some pretty aggressive treatment.' Amanda patted Carly on the shoulder. 'I can't do that here. She'll need to come back to the hospital with me.'

'But how?' Carly wailed. 'She can't even walk.'

'We'll have to float her. We'll just have to get her on her feet and drag her into a float, Carly,' Amanda said. I'd heard her use that tone with me. I knew what it meant. Destiny was in trouble. 'We don't have a choice.'

'No one's here to help me,' Carly sobbed. 'Who's gonna float her?'

'Becky? Becky, are you in here?'

'Dad!' Becky, sighed. 'Thank goodness.'

Gary stuck his head around the stable door. 'What's going on? I brought the float. It's right here by the stable, like you said. What's everyone doing here? Amanda, is that you? Good heavens, is that Destiny?'

Amanda took a few moments to fill Gary in. He shook his head and smacked his forehead with his hand. 'If only I'd been at the show. I could've done something.'

'Why didn't you come, Dad? I can't take it any more. All these secrets. It's not fair!' Becky was shaking.

Gary took his daughter in his arms and held her close. 'Not now, Beck. I'll tell you everything. But not now. We have to help Destiny, first and foremost.'

Becky nodded her agreement.

Amanda gave us instructions and the five of us worked together. Gary, Amanda, Carly, Becky and me. We pushed, pulled, tugged and heaved and eventually got Destiny to her feet. She was so hot. I'd never felt a horse so hot.

Gary pulled at her halter while Becky, Carly and I pushed her rump and Amanda supported her leg. It took a little while, but we got her into the float. Gary wasted no time securing Destiny and driving away with Carly in the back seat and Amanda following in her little blue four-wheel drive.

Becky and I were left standing there, both of us drained from the effort and the shock.

'What a nightmare,' I said. 'Poor Destiny. Poor Carly.'

'Let's hope she'll be okay. Destiny, that is.'

'Yeah.' I was exhausted. All I wanted to do was go home. I'd rest Honey, try to take it all in and get Mum or Dad to drive me to Amanda's surgery to visit Destiny. I'd take Carly something to eat. She sure looked like she could use it.

Becky and I tacked and mounted our horses, riding in the direction of home. I patted Honey's hard, sleek neck. She was healthy, strong and sound. I couldn't ask for anything more.

Mum was sitting at the front desk when I got home. She'd just finished checking in a couple to Guest Room 1. They looked tired. I smiled at them and Mum waved her hand at their bag. I knew what I had to do and picked it up. It was light, thank goodness.

'This came for you, Ash,' Mum said. She held out a letter.

I held it up to my face. Linley Heights School! They'd written back to me. Linley had never been for certain. They didn't have to take me. I was applying for a scholarship. I took the bag upstairs and put it down outside Guest Room 1. I could hear Savannah and Jenna giggling in my room. I needed somewhere quiet to read the letter and see what Linley had decided. There was only one place I could think of to read the letter. Honey's paddock.

I clutched the letter to my chest and ran back down the stairs, eager to share the news with Honey, whatever it happened to be.

twenty

New Beginnings

'How was the entrance exam?'

I knew Jenna was trying but I was over it. She'd dumped me for Savannah McMurray for the past week. The last thing I wanted to do was tell her about the Linley scholarship exam. Mum had driven me to the high school in town that morning, where kids from all over the region had come to sit for all kinds of scholarship exams into all kinds of high schools. I'd met a girl from Acacia Falls who was trying out for a music scholarship at Oxford Girls Grammar and a boy from Menidobar who was hoping for a tennis scholarship at Kings College. There had only been one other girl trying out for Linley on a riding scholarship. She'd looked me up and down and wished me luck.

The exam had been even more harrowing than the application form. I'd had to fill in pages of information about myself, my goals and riding achievements, and had to explain why I wanted to go to Linley. I'd faced a panel of four who'd asked me all kinds of questions about riding, and then I had to sit a three-hour academic exam in Maths and English. By the time I staggered from the room, my head felt like it had been balancing a bale of hay all day, and my brain felt like it had jumped through hoops of fire, but I didn't want to *bore* Jenna with all of that.

'Fine,' I said. I opened the fridge door and stared at its contents. Why is there never anything decent to eat when you're not really hungry? 'Where's your friend?'

Jenna half-smiled. 'Had a better offer for today. Look, Ash, I've only got a few days left. Why don't we do something special together?'

I shrugged. 'I dunno, Jen.'

'Oh c'mon, Ash. We used to have so much fun together. Doncha remember that garage sale? I'll never forget the look on your dad's face when you tried to sell him his own guitar.'

I smiled, in spite of myself. 'He reckons that's the day he got his first grey hair.'

'So whaddya say?'

I regarded her cautiously. Something about her was different. Good different this time. She wasn't wearing any make-up and she seemed to have forgotten her Italian.

'Jen, you can't just come back to me 'cause Savannah's busy. And if you hate it here that much you can always go home early. No one's forcing you to stay.'

Jenna nodded. 'I know. I've been doing some thinking.' She looked around the kitchen. 'This place, this B & B, it needs something. What d'you say I set up a website for Miller Lodge?'

I raised my eyebrows. 'A website? You mean you'd be using the computer for something other than chatting to your Italian friends?'

Jenna moaned. 'Gimme a break, Ash. I know I've been a bit, a bit weird.'

I shook my head. 'But I don't get it. Why are you normal all of a sudden? I've been living with a stranger for weeks and now you just flick a switch and you're you again?'

'I've been thinking. About you and that horse, Carly's horse.'

'About how I'm immature and she's smelly?' I knew I was giving her attitude, but I was hurt.

Jenna shook her head. 'No. It's just that I realized horses are who you are. I wanted to change you. I wanted to make you more like me. But you wouldn't be Ash any more and I really don't want that.'

'So we're still friends, even though I have a slight horse addiction?' I offered her my hand, hoping more than anything that she'd accept it.

'Just friends?' Jenna said, feigning shock. 'We're best friends, Ash. Always have been.' She grabbed my hand.

'Always will be.' I pulled her into a hug.

'You know, that Savannah,' Jenna said.

'What about her?' I held Jenna at arm's length and studied her face.

'She seems to be a bit, I dunno, competitive. Did you notice or is it just me?'

I cracked up laughing. It felt good after all the stress over Jenna and the exam. 'Ha! I figured Savannah McMurray out faster than you did. Ha!'

Jenna covered her ears with her hands. 'I never want to hear that word again!'

'Ha!' I cried. 'Ha, ha and ha!'

The doorbell rang. Jenna and I ran for it together, like nothing had ever happened between us. It was unreal.

I wrenched open the door, giggling. Becky was standing on the veranda, her hair in plaits, her helmet jammed on her head.

'What's going on?' she said, a smile tugging at her lips.

'Jenna is totally over Savannah McMurray,' I beamed.

'Ha!' Becky shrieked.

Jenna groaned and clutched her stomach. 'Not you, too!'

'Feel like checking on the patient?' Becky said.

Becky and I exchanged glances and I held my breath waiting for Jenna's reply. Her haircut was the same, she was still tall and slender, but was she really her old self again?

'You bet!' Jenna said.

The three of us fell into a cuddle.

'I still can't believe all this happened,' Becky said, sighing. We were squeezed into a stall at Amanda Filano's surgery stroking Destiny. She'd been on intravenous antibiotics and fluids for the last few days and was much better. Amanda had been right. Septicaemia. Destiny's blood had been poisoned by bacteria from the abscess. It was something you heard about, but never happened to a horse you knew.

'Hey, did your dad fess up? About Western?' I slung my arm over Destiny's back and looked into Becky's eyes.

'Eventually,' she said. 'It's a long story.'

'We've got time,' I said. 'Right, Jenna?'

Jenna checked her watch. 'All the time in the world.'

Becky ran her hand down Destiny's leg. 'The swelling's gone down. Thank goodness we have a vet like Amanda here. She's so good with horses.'

'But look at her hoof,' I said, pointing. 'It's like something's eaten a big hole in it.'

'It did,' Becky said. 'Doesn't smell as bad today.'

'If this isn't bad I'd hate to have smelled it before. It's foul!' Jenna held her nose.

'That's pus for you,' Becky said brightly.

I cleared my throat. 'Western riding? Your dad? Long story?'

'We're waiting,' Jenna said.

Becky sighed. 'Remember that horse Dad was riding in the old photos, Ash?'

I nodded. 'The chestnut Quarter Horse.'

'That's him. His show name was The Ultimate Dream, but Dad just called him Duke. He got him as a three-year-old and had him for years.'

'And you never knew about him?' Jenna was entranced.

Becky shook her head. 'Not a thing. Anyway, they were known around the district as an unbeatable show team. They won everything. Dad was even chosen to go to the States for the World Titles. But they never made it.'

'What happened?' I whispered. I almost didn't want to know any more.

Becky rubbed at her eyes. 'Dust,' she said.

But I knew better.

'They were in a reining class. Everything was going well. They did a sliding stop and Duke just landed wrong. Snapped his near hind hock. There was nothing anyone could do.'

'That's horrible,' I said. 'Really horrible.'

'Dad swore he'd never ride Western again. He blamed himself. He still does.' Becky sighed.

I felt sick then. For poor Gary and his horse and all the years he wasted feeling guilty and turning his back on the riding he loved.

'Do you think he'll ever compete again?' Jenna asked, her eyes wide.

'I hope so. For him, anyway.'

I held my hand out to Becky and she grabbed it. Jenna held Becky's other hand. We were a team. We knew we always would be.

'We need to celebrate,' I said, squeezing Becky's hand.

'What?' she said.

'New beginnings,' I smiled. 'And old friends.'

'And I think I know the perfect place and the perfect occasion.'

twenty-one

Party Time

'I gotta hand it to you, Ash. This is definitely the party of the year. How'd you pull it all together so fast?'

'The pony express is a wonderful thing, Preezy-Boo!' I hugged my best friend. Hey! I just said best friend. And why not? If I could have two I could surely have three. Three best friends. Each one different, but all as precious as Honey, and as much a part of my life. Jenna, Becky and Pree. They made my heart beat.

Becky joined us. Then Jenna. We surveyed the party room at Shady Trails Riding Ranch. It had been my dream to turn twelve right here in this room and sit on the Pegasus throne with a room full of my best friends eating at the horseshoe-shaped tables. I was back where I belonged at last.

'Did you straighten it all out with Mrs McMurray?' Pree asked, adjusting the party hat on her head.

'I did in the end.' I smiled. I'd missed Mrs Mac and Shady Trails so much. 'We were wrong to have doubted each other. That's what she said. And now that she believes all the gory details you told her about that trail ride, Savannah's the one banned from the Ranch.'

'They're flying home soon, aren't they?' Jenna said, nibbling daintily at an enormous slice of pizza.

'Not soon enough,' I grumbled. But then I shook my head and smiled. 'Not today. Today is all about fun.'

'And friends,' Becky said.

'And horses,' Pree added, a smile spread across her face.

'When are you going home, Jen?' Becky said.

Jenna smiled wistfully. 'Tomorrow morning. I don't really want to go now.'

'That's not what you said last week!' I said, wiggling my eyebrows.

Jenna groaned and covered her face with her hands. 'Don't remind me!'

'Don't worry, Jenna,' Becky said, a wicked grin plastered on her face. 'We won't go there, will we, *ragazzi*!'

The four of us fell apart laughing, our arms wrapped around each other. It was the best feeling in the world. I looked around the room, at the murals, the unicorns hanging from the ceiling, the throne and the horseshoe-shaped table with my birthday cake sitting proudly in the centre. But most of all I looked at the people. The room was filled with people. People I loved. People I needed. Good people. I saw Mrs McMurray on the other side of the room by the floor to ceiling window that looked out onto the holding yard and waved. She waved back and gave me one of her most special smiles. I laughed aloud, the joy I felt at being back at the Ranch on my birthday bursting out of me for everyone to see. I wanted it to last forever. Or to at least be like a favourite book whose pages I could turn to anytime. I was home. I was really home.

'Well, Miss Twelve-and-a-Day-Old,' Mum said, sitting on the edge of my bed. 'How does it feel to have your room back to yourself again?'

'Not so good,' I admitted. 'I miss Jenna. We lost so much time while she was here and now I probably won't see her again for ages. She's started on our website, by the way. But she said she'll finish it at home.'

'You never know.' Mum tucked a stray wisp of hair behind my ear. 'We have friends in the city. And Gran likes us to visit. We'll try to make it back soon, eh?'

'What about Honey and Toffee?' I'd never thought of leaving them. Not even for a minute, much less for a holiday.

'Later,' Mum said. 'We'll worry about that later.'

She pulled an envelope, long and white, out of her jacket and laid it on the bed. 'This just came for you. Looks rather official, don't you think?'

I picked it up and held it up close to my face. *Linley Heights School* was printed on the front of the envelope in neat silver letters.

'It's about the scholarship, isn't it?'

'Don't know,' Mum said, tapping my nose gently with the tip of her finger. 'But there's only one way to find out, possum.'

I held it tightly between my fingers. It was all here, inside this envelope. My whole future. Maybe they'd accepted me. If they had I'd be leaving Shady Creek with Honey and making a new home for us at the most awesome boarding school in the country, where I could study riding and Horsemanship and my dream of a life with horses would surely come true.

Or maybe they'd rejected me. Then I'd be going to Shady Creek and Districts High School next year with Becky and Pree. I wouldn't have world-class facilities at my fingertips, but I'd have my friends.

'I'm scared.' I folded up the envelope. 'I don't want to know.'

Mum patted my knee. 'Just open it. Whatever that letter says we'll deal with it. Dad and I will love and support you no matter what happens. No matter what you decide.'

'You'd probably love me more if I was at boarding school, though, right?'

'No doubt,' Mum said, without a moment's hesitation. 'One less mouth to feed and an extra room to let out. We'll be laughing!'

I whacked her with my pillow.

Dad stuck his head around the door then waltzed into my room with Jason in his arms. 'Well? Are we off to Linley? Or are me and Jase premature in our victory dance?'

'Dad!' I cried. 'What's with everyone? You really wanna get rid of me that badly?'

'Not really,' Dad said. 'We just need to know whether or not our application fee was well spent.'

'That's it!' I tore open the envelope and yanked out a folded piece of expensive paper.

'Let me see!' Mum made a grab at the paper but I snatched it away, then unfolded it slowly, enough to drive her crazy.

'Come on, Ash. What's it say?' Mum said.

I cleared my throat. '*Dear Ashleigh Miller.* Blah, blah, blah. *Careful consideration.* Blah, blah.'

'Don't *blah*!' Mum yowled. 'The blahs are usually the most important bits!'

I cackled. 'Okay, okay. *Dear Ashleigh Miller. After careful consideration, Linley Heights School—*'

'I can't take it any more,' Mum said, ripping the paper from my hands and poring over the words. 'Oh, Ash. It's a full scholarship! A full riding scholarship for the term of your secondary education.'

Dad grabbed the letter from Mum and was silent for a moment as he read. 'It's true.'

I jumped up and threw my arms around Mum's neck, laughing like a loon. Mum hugged me back and swung me around so fast that my feet left the floor.

'Excited?' Dad said, bouncing Jason in his arms.

'You bet,' I cried. 'Linley Heights School. It's a dream come true. Riding at school. Having Honey with me at school. And they picked me. Me!'

'It's wonderful, possum,' Mum said, holding me at arm's length and searching my eyes with hers.

'But wait,' I said, feeling suddenly that I was falling heavily from a Clydesdale's back. 'I have to leave home. I won't see you every day.'

Mum's eyes moistened. 'You'll be fine,' she said, sniffing and raising her chin. 'I promise you, Ash, you'll be just fine.'

'I can't believe it,' I said, flopping down on the bed. 'I can't believe it's really happening.'

'Neither can we, kid.' Dad sat on a part of the bed that wasn't taken up with me or Mum. Jason wriggled to the floor, lay on his tummy and chewed happily on the envelope.

'I reckon I'll miss you, Ash,' Dad said, tousling my hair.

'I don't have to go!' I said, sitting up. 'I can tell them thanks but no thanks. I can stay here with you and go to school in town. Everything can stay the same. Nothing has to change.'

'Things change all the time, possum,' Mum said. 'Just look at the last few weeks.'

She was right. Jenna had changed, then changed back. I'd lost Shady Trails then rediscovered it. Destiny's close call had changed things between Carly and me. Even if it had just been for one day. And now I was going to Linley Heights School.

'Just promise me one thing,' I said, looking solemnly at my parents.

'Tell us what it is first,' Mum said. 'Before we commit.'

'That you won't let out my room. Don't forget it's a gallery of timeless pieces of equine art.'

'Like the headless horse clock!' Mum and Dad said together.

'Right!' I wrapped my arms around them both and tickled Jason with my toes. I squeezed my parents, holding them as close as I could. I wanted to remember this always, this feeling. I wanted to take it out into the world with me and Honey and knock down every obstacle in our path. Linley Heights was just around the corner. And I couldn't wait to be part of it.

Glossary

barbie barbecue

bindi patch a collection of weed-like plants known for their sharp-needled seeds

biscuit Australian term for cookie

bowerbird an Australian bird that hoards shiny objects to create elaborate twig huts

brumby an Australian wild or feral horse

chucked up threw up

doover thingamabob or thingamajig

grottiest 'grossest'; most disgusting

gymkhana an equestrian event, usually for young people, that involves timed games for riders on horses

hack to 'go for a hack' means to go for a walk or a slow canter on a horse

interstate on business on a business trip to another state within Australia

joddies abbreviation for jodhpurs

lounge sofa

lucerne alfalfa

nappies diapers

no fear an expression indicating refusal or disagreement

ring to call on the telephone

switched on excited

Textas coloured felt pens

three bags full a slang expression used to describe a person who is fawning over another

Acknowledgements

I would like to thank my gorgeous children, Mariana, John and Simon — you are my inspiration. Seb, you are my guiding light; you make me want to write. To my family — Janet, George, Andy, Cassandra, Mike, Kaitlin, Hayley and Caleb — thank you for your unwavering love and support. Thanks and love to my beautiful friends, Lo'ani, Jenny, Juli and Vicki. Thanks also to Joanne Gregory and Suzi MacLaughlin for your advice on Western riding. And special thanks to Georgia, Appaloosa mare extraordinaire.

Photo by Dyan Hallworth

KATHY HELIDONIOTIS lives in Sydney and divides her time between writing stories, reading good books, teaching and looking after her three gorgeous children. Kathy has had twelve children's books published so far. *Horse Mad Western* is the fifth book in the popular Horse Mad series. Watch out for Book 6, *Horse Mad Heights*, coming soon.

Visit Kathy at her website:
www.kathyhelidoniotis.com

Also by Kathy Helidoniotis:

Totally Horse Mad
Horse Mad Summer
Horse Mad Academy
Horse Mad Heroes

Coming Soon
Horse Mad Heights

It's all about friendship, fun and a passion for horses

Totally Horse Mad

by Kathy Helidoniotis

Totally Horse Mad

The only things that stand between Ashleigh Miller and the horse of her dreams are a whole lot of dollars that she doesn't have, parents who don't know one end of a horse from another and a city backyard the size of a shoebox.

Ashleigh can't believe it when her parents announce that she will really have a horse of her own, but at a price she could never have imagined. She will have to say goodbye to her best friend, Jenna, South Beach Stables and her favourite horse, Princess. Ashleigh and her family are leaving the city and heading for Shady Creek, a small country town. And that's where the adventures in this Horse Mad series really begin.

Horse Mad Summer

Ashleigh is itching for her Horse Mad holiday with Beck and Jenna to begin. Her two best friends will be meeting each other for the first time and she's sure all three of them will have the best summer together.

But when Jenna finally arrives from the city, Ashleigh feels like the ham in the sandwich. Torn between spending time with Jenna and helping her with her riding lessons and also keeping an eye on the Creepketeers with Becky, Ashleigh's dream holiday isn't turning out as she'd hoped. The situation gets worse when Jenna confides in Ash and makes her promise not to tell anyone — not even Becky. With the secret threatening to tear them all apart, can Ashleigh bring her two best friends together before the summer is over?

Standards are high at the riding academy. Can Ashleigh and Honey make the grade?

Horse Mad Academy

By Kathy Helidoniotis

Horse Mad Academy

The Junior Cross-Country Riding Championships are over and Ashleigh Miller has arrived at Waratah Grove Riding Academy. It's a dream come true for any Horse Mad kid, but as Ashleigh discovers, things don't always turn out like you hope they will.

With a gruelling riding schedule, training with the best junior riders in Australia, and a horse who just refuses to do dressage, Ash is shocked when she finally begins to unravel Honey's mysterious past. Does she have what it takes to help her horse heal her soul? And with tensions between the riders also running high, Ashleigh is beginning to think that life in Shady Creek with the Creepketeers is simple.

Cassata has gone missing, but Ash and Becky are determined to find the beautiful mare

Horse Mad Heroes

by Kathy Helidoniotis

Horse Mad Heroes

Ashleigh is back from Waratah Grove and is excited to have landed a job at Shady Trails Riding Ranch, a new riding school that has opened in Shady Creek. But rivalry between Riding Club and the new school pits her against her best friend Becky for the first time. There's also a baby due any day now and with all the baby talk at home, Ash feels alone more than ever.

When Cassata, the beautiful Appaloosa mare goes missing, Ash and Becky are reunited. But will their quest to find Cassata be enough to heal their friendship?